A GLIMPSE of GLORY

SHANDI CARRIER

Ruach & Ember Press

A Glimpse of Glory
© 2025 by Shandi Carrier
All rights reserved.

ISBN (Paperback): 979-8-9998144-0-1
ISBN (eBook): 979-8-9998144-1-8
Library of Congress Control Number: 2025919481

Published by Ruach & Ember Press, Nashua, NH
Printed in the United States of America

To my husband, Shane, my greatest supporter and encourager.

And to my daughter, Birdi, the light who inspires
me to dream big and never give up.

A LETTER TO THE READER

This story addresses sensitive topics, including suicide,
abuse, and grief. These themes are handled with care and
ultimately point toward the hope and redemption found
in Christ. Please take care of your heart as you read.

Dear Reader,

If you're holding this book, I first want to say: thank you! No matter the reason you picked it up, I'm so glad you're here.

This story was written from a deep place in my heart. It explores pain, grief, and feeling alone. I know what it's like to wrestle with hard questions, especially the ones we're too afraid to say out loud.

But more than anything, this story is about hope. It's about light breaking through darkness. It's about Jesus leaving the ninety-nine to go after the one. And you're the one.

It's about discovering that you're never too far gone, never too broken, and more seen and loved than you realize.

If you've ever felt like Sammy—hurt, exhausted, unsure if life is worth living—I want you to know: you are not alone. I've been there too. You are deeply loved by a God who sees every tear you cry, hears every silent prayer, and knows your entire story, even the parts you haven't lived yet.

He's not afraid of your questions. Cry them out. Scream them out. If you read the Psalms, you'll see that God's people did the same. He welcomes your pain, your doubts, your honesty.

This book is not meant to glorify suicide. If you've ever felt like ending your life is the only option, please hear this: that is not the voice of your Savior. That is not the end of your story. There is a Savior who meets you in your lowest moment and promises to carry you through. He is the God of hope. And He has not forgotten you.

If you've lost someone to suicide, I am so deeply sorry. That pain is unlike any other. It's confusing, devastating, and full of questions that may never be answered this side of Heaven. Please know their life mattered. Their pain was real. And so is yours.

Jesus is close to the brokenhearted. He sees your pain, carries your sorrow, and walks with you through the questions. You are not alone.

If you're struggling, talk to someone. Reach out to a friend, a pastor, a counselor. You don't have to carry this alone. There is help. There is healing. And there is hope.

With love,
Shandi

IF YOU NEED HELP

If you or someone you love is struggling with thoughts of suicide, depression, or overwhelming pain—please reach out. You are not alone, and there is help available:

988 Suicide & Crisis Lifeline (USA)
Call or text **988** or visit 988lifeline.org
Free, confidential support 24/7.

BetterHelp
Access professional online therapy from licensed counselors anytime, anywhere.
Visit www.betterhelp.com

National Alliance on Mental Illness (NAMI)
Call **1-800-950-NAMI (6264)** or visit nami.org/help

To Write Love on Her Arms
Find hope and local mental health resources at twloha.com/find-help

Focus on the Family Counseling
Call **1-855-771-HELP (4357)** for a free, one-time consultation with a licensed Christian counselor.
Visit focusonthefamily.com

Note: The resources listed here are provided for informational purposes only. I do not control or endorse all of the content found through these organizations. Please use wisdom and discernment as you seek help and support.

*"Have I not commanded you? Be strong and courageous.
Do not be frightened, and do not be dismayed, for
the Lord your God is with you wherever you go."*

JOSHUA 1:9, ESV

CHAPTER 1

"For this light momentary affliction is preparing for us
an eternal weight of glory beyond all comparison."

2 Corinthians 4:17 esv

My feet feel like lead as I walk to the calendar hanging on the wall beside my bed. My body is weak. I can barely lift the marker. With what little strength I have, I draw a bright red X through Monday.

Just six boxes left.

I turn sharply toward the door. Loud sounds echo from downstairs.

Slam! One cabinet door.

Slam! Slam! There go two more.

Uh-oh. This can't be good.

"Samantha! Get down here! Now!"

At the sound of her voice, my body tenses. My hands start to shake.

I can hear my heart pounding in my ears. Nausea rises in my throat, and I feel lightheaded like I might pass out.

I take a few deep breaths to steady myself. That's as long as I dare take—any longer and she'll start yelling again.

I toss the marker down and make my way downstairs, head low.

I turn the corner into the living room, my feet leading while every instinct tells me to run the other way.

Too late. I come face to face with my mother. And she's not just angry. She's in one of her rages.

I stand still, hands clenched in front of me. Lifting my chin, I take a slow breath and meet her eyes.

"I told you just this morning if you see dishes in the sink, clean them!" Her icy stare cuts right through me.

"And now there's mud all over the floor. I know I wasn't the one who tracked it in."

She storms over to me until she's standing directly in front of me, arms crossed, her perfectly manicured nails tapping impatiently against her arm.

"I'm not asking for much, Samantha. When I was your age, I was taking care of everything. If I ever acted the way you do, I would've been punished—severely."

She grabs my arms, her voice rising. "You have no idea how easy you have it."

I wince, her grip too tight. I avoid her eyes and stare at the hardwood floor, waiting for her to finish.

She lets go of my arms, but she's not done. She pivots to her next complaint. I rub my arms, trying to erase the crescent-shaped imprints her fingernails left behind.

She walks over to the counter and leans against it, her eyes darkening. "Stop that, I barely touched you."

I let my arms fall to my sides.

"I got a call from your teacher today, Mr. Jones. He said he's been sending letters home, but none of them have come back signed. Care to explain that? Your teacher shouldn't have to call. Oh—and apparently, you're failing algebra."

My face turns red at being caught. I thought if I hid the letters, it would give me some time to turn my grade around before Mother found out. I peek up just in time to catch the look of disgust on her face.

"Don't you want a good life? You need better grades if you want a good job. You're running out of time. Graduation's not that far off, and you don't even have a plan!"

I bite my tongue to keep from responding. Any explanation will be called an excuse. There's nothing left for me to do but try to escape my living nightmare and retreat somewhere deep in my mind, where I'm free and happy.

. . .

There's a bright kitchen with fresh flowers on the table and the smell of freshly baked breakfast filling the air. My mother greets me with a hug and a kiss. She smiles at me with proud eyes and asks how I slept last night. My father is sitting at the table with a newspaper and a cup of coffee. He looks up and says, "Good morning, Sunshine," before turning to my mother and giving her a wink that makes me blush, feeling as though I've just witnessed a private moment.

My heart sinks as I pull myself out of my happy place, scolding myself for going there. Back to a time that once existed but now only serves as a painful reminder that life will never be the same.

"I don't know what you're thinking, but once you graduate, you're on your own. I had to figure it out, and so will you."

She huffs. "And unless your grades measure up, don't expect us to waste our money on college."

She whispers it under her breath, but I still catch what she says. *Why can't you be more like Stephen?*

The familiar ache wells up in my chest at the mention of my brother. She knows exactly how much that would hurt to hear—*but she's right.*

My brother wouldn't be failing them. He never failed at anything. He was the perfect child. And if he were here right now, this nightmare wouldn't be happening. *We'd still be the perfect family we once were.*

Stephen's death haunts me every single day. Every time I walk by his room, hear my mother sobbing when she thinks no one is listening, see his girlfriend at the supermarket, or when a single memory of our past flashes in my mind—I'm reminded that he's not here. And that life will never be the same.

• • •

Don't go there… please don't go there.

My mind drifts back to two years ago.

He was eighteen and only a couple of weeks away from graduating high school. Even from a young age, Stephen showed remarkable potential. He was a straight-A student, volunteered with local charities, and was a friend to everyone. He was my biggest role model. We had our moments, of course. I was the annoying little sister, and he was the older brother who liked to give me a hard time. But he always found ways to make sure I knew he loved me.

My favorite memory was when he would take me to the park, and we'd toss the football for hours. Thanks to him, I had a pretty good throw by the time I was twelve, which always surprised the boys at school.

Stephen was the guy who had a five-year plan. He was going to be an engineer. He planned on marrying his beautiful girlfriend after college, they would live in a little white house on the outskirts of town, and they would have a big family. There wasn't a single doubt in my mind that he would accomplish everything he set out to do.

But life had other plans.

Two years ago, Stephen died in a car accident.

Images of that night flash in my mind. Our parents had to work late, so Stephen was bringing me home from soccer practice. We were listening to our favorite song, sipping on milkshakes, when a deer ran out into the middle of the road.

Stephen slammed the brakes and swerved to miss the deer, but he overcorrected. The tires skidded off the shoulder and the car slid into Megunticook Lake.

We were trapped in a car that quickly filled with ice-cold water. He finally managed to break the back window after we were almost fully submerged and crawled out. He motioned for me to follow, thinking I was right behind him, and went up for air.

But my foot was stuck.

Stephen came back to get me.

He had asthma, so holding his breath had always been difficult for him. He finally got me loose after what felt like an eternity, and I swam to the surface as the car sank further into the lake.

Stephen never came up.

The exertion of breaking the glass, swimming out, then back to get me, and pulling me from the car had been too much for his lungs. He drowned.

Red and blue lights reflected on the lake as divers pulled Stephen's body from the water.

My parents arrived on the scene just as they covered him with a tarp. That was the first and last time I ever heard my father cry. My mother was inconsolable. She didn't speak to anyone that night. Her sobs were the only sound you could hear.

The crash of a plate snaps me back to reality. Shards scatter across the floor.

"Listen to me!" she yells, eyes wild with rage.

I flinch, then stammer out the only words I can find.

"I'm—I'm sorry."

I clear my throat, trying to steady my voice.

"I really am trying. But there's just no time. Between school and studying—"

I shake my head. "I rush home and try to get everything done, but it's never enough."

My mind scrambles for the right thing to say.

"My tutor said I'm doing better, though. He thinks I'll have it down soon. I promise I'll keep trying."

She slams her hand on the counter.

"Enough! I'm sick of your excuses." Her voice cuts like a blade.

"I worked too hard to become successful. I did eight years of schooling to become a dentist. Your father did seven to become a lawyer."

She glares at me. "If you want to be a nobody, do it somewhere else. Not in this house. We've sacrificed too much for you to mess it all up."

Sighing sharply, she asks, "Does that make sense, or do I need to say it again?"

I hear her loud and clear. I've understood since the first day she screamed at me—the day after Stephen died. It's very clear I will never live up to her expectations, and that she lost her only perfect child.

"I—I understand," I stammer.

My anxiety catches up to me again, and as much as I try to keep my composure, my old stutter keeps slipping through.

"Why are you stuttering? All those years of expensive speech lessons, and you're still talking like a baby."

She shakes her head, smooths down her skirt, and turns to leave.

But just before she disappears into her room, she stops.

With a sigh, she says, "Try harder, Samantha. You're all we have left."

Her words are meant to sound loving, but all they do is make me sick. The pressure is crushing.

I'm hoping that's the end of it. But before I can even catch my breath, she says the words I fear most.

"There's nothing for dinner for you. Head upstairs."

The words hit like a slap. I try not to show how much it hurts and turn toward the stairs, feeling defeated.

"Samantha, wait."

For a split second, hope flickers.

"Clean up the broken dish. Then go upstairs and study. I'll be up shortly to see if what you said about algebra is actually true. If you fail this quiz, there's no breakfast tomorrow. Food is for those who tell the truth."

My eyes start to water, but I will the tears to stay put. The last time I cried in front of my mother, she told me to stop, that crying made my face red and it wasn't becoming.

She's taken food from me before, but lately it's happening more often. At first, it was just here and there after Stephen died. But in the past year, things have gotten worse. She started staying home from work more, locking herself in her room, only coming out to eat on occasion. And when she did come out, she always found something to get angry about, which often led to her taking away my food privileges. Lunch is the only real meal I can depend on. And that's only because it's served at school.

How am I supposed to focus on school when my stomach feels like it's eating itself?

My head starts to ache. Taking a deep breath, I tell myself to pull it together. *If I can just pass this quiz—that I'm sure every other kid is being forced to take randomly at home—then I can have breakfast.*

I torture myself by picturing the most scrumptious pancakes smothered in butter and fresh syrup. Maybe some strawberries and whipped cream too. And a tall glass of fresh orange juice. Unfortunately, even if I do get to eat breakfast, it'll just be oatmeal. With my choice of side: banana or apple. Mother claims it's because she wants us to "stay healthy."

Truthfully, my mother looks like she could've been a model in her younger years—even now, with her long, shiny blonde hair and a body that stayed fit even after two kids. She would never let her daughter look anything less than perfect. So healthy food is the only option.

I clean up the broken plate, making sure to get every last shard. The work is tedious, and tears threaten to burn my eyes. I toss the remains into the trash, wash the dishes in the sink, wipe up the drop of mud by the front door, and quietly retreat to my room.

Closing the door as quietly as I can, I slide down against it, bury my head in my hands, and let the weight of my next decision settle in my chest like a stone.

This has to end.

CHAPTER 2

*C*ome on, Sam. You know this.

My palms are sweaty, and the pencil keeps slipping from my fingers as I frantically try to solve the algebra equations. The numbers blur on the page. I rub my eyes, trying to focus. The room starts to spin. My heart pounds.

My breathing becomes erratic. I clutch my head.

Focus, Sam.

I glance at the clock. Mother will be here any minute. I scribble down an answer to the last problem, something about factoring polynomials. I know it's wrong, but I'm out of time. I hear the click of her heels downstairs. I stand, paper in hand, shaking.

The doorknob turns slowly. My heart races faster.

She walks in, takes the paper from my hands, and leaves without a word.

A few minutes later, she storms back in, my quiz fluttering in her hand. Without saying anything, she drops it on the table.

Circled in red: **85**.

My stomach sinks. To anyone else, that would be a good grade. But I know what this means.

I failed.

The last question is marked wrong.

I was so close. Why couldn't I get it right?

She doesn't say a word. Just looks at me with pure disappointment, turns, and walks out.

I hear the door click shut. Then—

Click.

The lock.

Her heels grow quieter with each step.

The sound of my only way out walking away.

Looks like no breakfast for me.

We have a rule in our house that anything below a 90 is failing. My teachers have always praised me for maintaining high grades, except for math, which has always been my weak spot. What they don't know is that lately, I don't have a choice. In order to eat, I need to get perfect grades. *It's not a choice anymore. It's my only way to survive.*

Frustrated and starving, I collapse onto my bed and stare at the ceiling. My eyes burn, but the tears won't come anymore. I've cried too much over the last two years. Every morning when I wake, I tell myself I'm going to be brave. I'm going to be strong. And I won't cry my life away.

But they just kept coming—until tonight.

Tonight, the tears have dried up, and my heart is hardening. Anger swirls inside me like black sludge, and I let it. *I'd rather feel anger than pain.*

It wasn't always like this. I wasn't always sad. Mother wasn't always mean. I had a family once. A family that loved one another. We were happy.

Once Stephen died, my father buried himself in work. He practically lives at his office now and rarely comes home. I often hear my mother yelling at him on the phone, and it's no wonder he doesn't want to come back. In his effort to avoid her wrath, he's abandoned me—his only daughter.

Every once in a while, I get a text that says, "Work will slow down soon, and I'll be home." But I know he only sends those because he feels guilty. Work never slows down. And he never intends to come home.

● ● ●

Failing today's quiz reminds me of the moment I knew everything had changed.

A couple months after Stephen died, I was desperate. I didn't finish my chores the day before and had just gotten a 70 on a math test.

Mother told me there'd be no food for me that day, *not until your grade is back to an A,* she said. A whole day without eating. I was starving.

I remember pacing my room, clutching my phone. *Please Dad, answer.*

"Samantha." His voice was distracted. I could hear voices in the background.

"Um… hey, Dad, I was—"

"What is it, Samantha? I'm in the middle of a meeting."

"It's Mom," I rushed out. "She won't let me eat."

Silence.

"Dad? Are you still there?"

"Samantha, I told you. I'm in a meeting. I'll call you back later. Bye."

Call Ended.

He never called me back.

That was the last time I ever called him.

And the last time I would ever let him hurt me again.

. . .

I stuff the memory deep down, like I've learned to do. Instead, I let my mind drift back to a time when I felt safe, when I felt loved. Back to my childhood. It all feels like a fantasy now. Growing up in midcoast Maine was a child's dream. The rocky shoreline, wild and untamed, felt forbidden, but it called my name with the crashing of its waves. The towering pines, which to a young girl's eyes seemed to stretch into the heavens, filled my heart with wonder.

Our family often hiked together or walked along the beach after dinner. Living in a place this beautiful made me dream of seeing the world. *If Maine could be this magical, imagine what else was out there.*

It was always Mom, Dad, Stephen, and me. And Lucky, our two-year-old cocker spaniel. He was a stunning dog, with the shiniest fur and floppy ears that bounced as he ran alongside us. We were happy. Until Stephen died.

Shortly after, Mother gave Lucky away. She said she was developing allergies to dogs, which didn't make sense—we'd already had him for two years. Despite all my begging and crying, she dropped him off at a shelter. She told me to stop crying, that it wouldn't be fair to keep a dog who made her sick.

I knew the real reason why she got rid of Lucky. We always joked that he was Stephen's dog because we got him on Stephen's birthday. He never left Stephen's side; he even slept in his bed every night. After Stephen died, the night he passed, Lucky paced in front of his door for hours, pawing at it to be let in.

My mother didn't let anyone into Stephen's room after that night, but that didn't stop Lucky from trying. I think it was too painful for her to watch, knowing the door would never open again. I tried to get Lucky to stop, but he wouldn't.

That's why my mother gave him away.

Between Stephen's death and Father's absence, Mother changed. Grief turned her into someone unrecognizable. For the last two years, I've been the only one left around her and I've become her emotional punching bag.

Daydreaming got me into trouble, but I enjoyed thinking back on those earlier days and filling my mind with wonderful memories.

One of my favorite memories was a camping trip when I was ten and Stephen was fifteen. Every night was filled with marshmallows, campfire stories, and gazing at the stars.

I loved the stars. My father used to point out all the different planets and constellations. I was always so impressed that he knew all of them. Well, it seemed like he did.

He was also a great storyteller. In vivid detail, he would tell us the folklore of the White Mountains in New Hampshire (another spot where our family loved to camp), or his favorite, about the ghosts in Vermont.

I never felt scared though. I sat snuggled up next to my father as he told those stories, and it was the safest I have ever felt.

It's been a long time since I've felt that.

Stephen would get involved in the stories and act out scenes. Mother would look around at all of us and smile. She was so happy then. I would do anything to get that family back.

I glance at my nightstand and pick up the photo of me and Stephen. The frame is chipped on one corner from when I dropped it a few months ago, but I never replaced it.

On the back, in his familiar handwriting, are the words: *You got this, kid.*

It used to make me feel strong. Now, it just makes me ache.

That life feels like it belonged to someone else.

I think back to the conversations from earlier this evening. Mother wasn't entirely wrong. Why couldn't I be more like Stephen—smart, popular, good-looking? Compared to the other girls in my grade, I still haven't caught up. I'm taller than most of them, but my body still looks like a twelve-year-old boy's.

Who could ever love someone like me?

I used to have dreams until my parents started planning my future for me. I wanted to be a journalist. I had always enjoyed writing and even won a couple of contests. Mother and Father seemed so proud then. But something changed after Stephen died.

Maybe they always assumed Stephen would be the one to be successful and weren't paying too much attention to me. But now that I'm the only one left, the pressure to succeed has only intensified.

I would've traveled the world and written exciting pieces about other cultures. But Mother says I have to be "more realistic." She's decided I'll work in accounting even though I hate math. She says it's my only shot in life, and Father agrees that it'll be a stable job.

The reality of my future leaves me feeling more frustrated than afraid. But I don't have to worry about it much longer—

Because I've decided: in seven days, I'm going to kill myself.

May 3rd. Just a date on the calendar. But to me, it's a finish line.

. . .

I sigh and put the picture in my nightstand drawer. The drawer catches as I try to close it.

I pull out a folded photo that's been wedged into the side.

It's a picture of me and two of my best friends. *Former best friends.* The three of us are laughing, frozen in a moment that feels like another lifetime.

I won't have to worry about them missing me. I don't have friends anymore. My mother made sure of it. She said friends are a distraction. That I need to focus on what matters.

My life is now: school, after-school tutoring, cleaning, not eating, repeat.

I still don't understand why she thinks not eating will somehow motivate me to work harder. If anything, I can't focus. But to Mother, that's tough love. And tough love conquers all. Ha. I used to believe love conquered all. Isn't that what they say in church, anyway?

Growing up, we faithfully went to church. I could tell you all about Jesus, and God, and Moses, and Noah, and all the characters of the Bible. But that's just it—they're characters. Nothing more.

If God was real, my brother wouldn't have died that night.

If God was real, I wouldn't be locked in my room, starving, because I got an eighty-five on a test.

If God was real, my life wouldn't feel like this.

I used to believe he was real. But I don't anymore.

In seven days, I'll be gone. No bright light. No fire and brimstone. Just silence.

And finally freedom.

CHAPTER 3

*"For we are the aroma of Christ to God among those who
are being saved and among those who are perishing, to one
a fragrance from death to death, to the other a fragrance
from life to life. Who is sufficient for these things?"*

2 Corinthians 2:15-16 esv

It's foggy this morning, but the sun is trying to break through. The fog feels like the perfect mirror for my mood.

This morning, I really try. I wear my favorite pink blouse, the one that actually fits me right. I hope it might spark a memory in my mother, take her back to when I was little and always wore pink dresses to our tea parties. Back when she calls me her little angel. I even spend twenty minutes twisting my hair into a ballerina bun, hoping that maybe, if I try hard enough, she'll let me eat breakfast.

No such luck.

The moment she sees me, she scoffs, yanks a white shirt from the closet, and tells me to "Do better."

So I change. Bite my tongue to keep from begging. And walk out the door.

Hungry. Again.

Five minutes later, the bus arrives. The creaky door opens, and I step in.

The bus goes silent the moment I walk on, and I know why. There's no hiding how ghostly I look these days. I'm 5'6" and barely weigh 100 pounds. Just this past year, I've lost 25. My cheekbones jut out, and my skin stretches too tightly across my face, giving it an almost translucent look.

No matter how much makeup I wear, I can't cover the deep shadows beneath my eyes. My hair has started falling out from the stress at home, and probably from the lack of food. Thinning spots have started to show through, and I do my best to hide them. Wearing my hair up helps disguise how bad it's gotten.

I keep my head down and move quickly, searching for an empty seat, just trying to disappear.

Whispers trail behind me as I pass.

"What's wrong with her?" I hear one boy mutter.

"Look how skinny she is. Is she bulimic?" another girl snickers from the front—the group of popular girls who've always had something cruel to say, even back when I used to be "normal."

Their words don't sting as much anymore. After a while, it just becomes routine.

But then comes a different kind of whisper.

"I kind of feel bad for her."

I stop abruptly beside the row where I heard the whisper.

It's Jenny and Jessica, the girls from the picture.

They used to be my best friends. Ever since we were little, it was always the three of us. We were inseparable. But after Stephen died, my mother started keeping me from them, forbidding me from hanging out or even texting. Over time, our friendship faded. Even at school, I didn't know how to explain what was happening. So, I shut down. I kept everyone out. The pain was too overwhelming, and I didn't want anyone to see how much it hurt.

I overheard them once, saying I'd turned into a different person, and that it was hard to be friends with me anymore. They were right. I did turn into a different person. I didn't have a choice. My life is now ruled by an overbearing, cruel mother who makes sure I am just as miserable as she is.

But I miss them. So much.

We used to have sleepovers every weekend, staying up until one in the morning, drinking soda, and eating way too much candy. I'd always wake up feeling sick the next day, but I'd give anything to feel that again. To feel normal. To feel wanted.

My eyes lock with Jessica's, then Jenny's. They both look away, cheeks flushed, suddenly very interested in their shoes.

I stare at them for too long, and the kids around us start to snicker at the awkward exchange. I keep walking to the back where I know there's an empty bench just for me.

As soon as I sit down the commotion resumes and the kids laugh and gossip like they always do. I sigh and look out the window as the bus bumps down the road, wondering what it would feel like to be carefree again.

My finger finds a spot of chipping paint beneath the window, and I start picking at it, letting my mind wander.

A couple of houses down from mine, the bus stops. *That's odd. Nobody lives there.* The door opens, and everyone stops what they're doing to look up and see who's getting on.

My heart starts beating louder and faster, and I'm not sure why.

My breath catches in my throat, and I find myself half-standing to get a better look.

I'm confused to see an average fifteen-year-old boy. I'm not sure what I was expecting, but with the strange way my heart is racing and how the air seemed to shift, I definitely wasn't expecting someone so… normal.

He's maybe six feet tall with wavy brown hair that falls to his shoulders, looking like it could use a good wash. His height makes him walk slightly hunched over. His shirt has a stain at the bottom, and his jeans are ripped—not in the store-bought way, but in the natural, worn-in way before it became a trend.

He fumbles the book he's holding, quickly snatching it back up. As he walks toward the back of the bus, his eyes meet mine—they light up.

A flicker of joy flashes across his face, which is wild because I've never seen this boy in my life.

All eyes are on him, and silence fills the bus. It feels like we're all under a spell. Time seems to slow, and warmth fills the air. This strange feeling of calmness wraps around me, and for a moment, I believe everything will be okay.

Suddenly, he's standing in front of me and time catches up with us. The kids resume their chatter and laughter, moving on from this strange new boy.

"Can I sit here?" he asks, and yet I can't seem to speak. I simply nod my head and move my backpack out of the way. Scooting as close to the window as possible, I try to create distance. I'm confused about what just happened and don't want to be any closer to this new kid than I have to be.

He stares at me for a moment, and the kindness in his brown eyes makes me uncomfortable. I get the strange feeling that I know him, even though I've never seen him before. The sense of calm that settles over me just being near him only makes me more uneasy.

He interrupts my thoughts.

"Hey, I'm Joshua," he says with a half-smile.

He stares at me, waiting for me to respond.

I freeze, feeling painfully self-conscious. My mind goes blank. He's still waiting, and my brain refuses to cooperate. Finally, I blurt out, "I'm Sam—Samantha."

My face burns. *Of course I stuttered.* My mother would be furious if she saw this, though she'd wait until we were in private to say anything.

Joshua doesn't seem to mind. He smiles so big his eyes crinkle, and it's infectious. I can't help but smile back. I can't remember the last time I smiled.

"Samantha… Sammy," he says, pausing as if testing the name.

"Does anyone call you Sammy? I like it."

He smiles, then adds, "Thanks for letting me sit with you. First day on the bus is kind of scary."

He chuckles nervously.

"You're welcome." My voice feels stuck in my throat.

He called me Sammy. The last person who called me that was Stephen.

I try again, this time managing a full sentence.

"It doesn't matter. Most people call me Samantha or Sam. But… I like Sammy too."

Joshua smiles that infectious smile again, seeming pleased with himself.

"I just moved here last week. It's been a whirlwind."

He gives a nervous laugh.

"I've been extremely anxious about today, wondering if anyone would like me… if I'd make any new friends. All my best friends are back home."

He glances away, then adds quietly, "We actually got together before I left and prayed that God would send me a new friend right away."

He pauses, then chuckles.

"And I think my prayer just got answered."

I turn and look at him, confused.

What did he just say?

He was praying for a friend… and now he thinks that's me?

This kid's definitely religious. A Bible thumper, maybe. Fantastic. Just what I need.

I should probably set him straight before he gets any ideas.

"It was nice meeting you, Joshua, but I don't really do the whole religion thing. No offense."

I feel kind of bad for being so blunt and rude, but I don't need some person telling me about God.

God has done nothing for me. I'm not interested in him.

Joshua doesn't look hurt or shocked. Instead, with kind eyes and his smile still intact, he nods, turns away, and opens up his book.

Which is, of course, *The Bible.*

My face turns red and I look around, hoping no one is paying attention to us. But the other kids don't seem to notice the weird boy sitting with the weird girl.

For once, I'm thankful for being mostly invisible.

I check the time on my watch, twenty more minutes until we arrive at school. My stomach starts making noises, and I press my books against it, hoping to muffle the sound. I don't want "Bible Boy" over here to notice. He'll probably assume, just like everyone else, that Samantha is anorexic, or bulimic, or whatever rumor is going around now.

Another loud grumble escapes, and my face flushes with heat. I quickly look out the window, hoping Bible Boy didn't hear it.

I jump a little when something lands in my lap. *A granola bar.*

I glance over and see Joshua looking at me. There's no pity in his eyes, just kindness.

"Looks like you forgot to eat breakfast too," he says casually. "I'm always procrastinating in the mornings and never have time to eat. I grabbed two granola bars today. You can have my extra one. I hate when my stomach's growling during class. It's the worst."

I mumble, "Thank you," and unwrap it. *Apple cinnamon. Yum. I haven't had one of these since I was a kid.* I savor each bite, grateful I won't spend the next four hours trying to silence a growling stomach. I eat every last crumb and nearly consider licking the wrapper, but I don't want to give away just how desperate I really am.

Now I'm feeling extra embarrassed about how I treated Bible Boy earlier.

"Thanks for the granola," I say quietly. "But... why are you being so nice to me? Especially after I was rude to you. Sorry about that, by the way."

Joshua laughs. "Why wouldn't I be nice? You're a person. You matter."

He blushes a little. "My mom always says I don't have a filter. I just say what's on my mind. As for earlier, sorry if it came out creepy... about praying for a friend and that it's already been answered."

His blush deepens, and for some reason, that makes me relax. I'm not the only one feeling nervous.

"I was really nervous about moving," he admits. "I wasn't exactly the cool kid at my last school, so I didn't know if I'd make any friends here."

He shrugs slightly.

"But then I saw you sitting in the back of the bus... and I don't know. Something felt familiar. Like I was supposed to sit there."

He glances at me. "I just felt drawn to you."

I stare at him, my face warming at the thought that someone actually saw me—and wanted to be my friend.

We start chatting about where he's from, his family, and what he likes to do for fun, which is mainly basketball and skateboarding. He spends a good ten minutes talking about his love of skateboarding, his face lighting up with every word.

I get lost in his happiness. For a moment, I forget about my problems.

He just moved here from California. It was a big change moving to the East Coast, but his dad got a new job and they had to relocate.

Before I know it, the bus rolls up in front of the school.

Joshua glances past me out the window.

"We're already here?" He laughs, rubbing the back of his neck.

"I can't believe I talked the entire time. I didn't even let you get a word in."

He doesn't know I've mastered the art of getting people to talk. It's easier that way. In all honesty, I don't want to talk about my life. I'd have to lie—like always. *Oh, my mother and father are the greatest, they care about me and want the best for me, blah blah blah.* It's easier if they talk and I listen. I can immerse myself in their world for a moment and forget about mine.

We step off the bus and I start walking toward the school entrance when Joshua falls in step beside me, shooting me one of those charming half-grins. My lips tug upward before I can stop them.

There's overflowing joy in his eyes and I want to steal just a little for myself. *He must have an easy life to be that happy.*

"I gotta get to my first class," I say to Joshua. "The principal's office is down the hall and to the left. You'll probably need to check in there since you're new."

I quickly start walking away, but Joshua's long legs catch up to me with ease. He gently places his hand on my shoulder to slow me down.

"Hey, Sammy, it was nice talking with you," he says, glancing away for a moment like he's weighing his next words. When he looks back, something about his expression shifts. He suddenly looks… uneasy. And that makes me uneasy.

"You know how I said I don't really have a filter, and I just say what's on my mind?" he asks. "Well… I feel like God wants me to tell you something. I don't know why, and it might sound super weird, but I just need to say it."

He pauses, takes a deep breath, then says softly, "All the pain and mess we deal with down here? It's nothing compared to the glory waiting for us one day."

His hand drops from my shoulder. I hadn't even realized it was still there.

"Hopefully that means something to you," he says with a small shrug. "It was really nice meeting you. See you around."

He flashes that big grin again and bounds off toward the principal's office, leaving me standing in the hallway, stunned. His strange words echo in my mind, striking a chord deep in my heart I didn't expect.

CHAPTER 4

*"Come to me, all who labor and are
heavy laden, and I will give you rest."*
Matthew 11:28 esv

I'm jostled by kids rushing past me, a few muttering for me to get out of the way. But I can't. My feet feel glued to the floor as Joshua's words loop in my mind. *It's nothing compared to the glory waiting for us one day.* The first warning bell rings, sharp and jarring, snapping me out of my thoughts. I don't have time to process what just happened. If I don't move fast, I'll be late for class.

I rush into Creative Writing. It's the one elective I had to beg my mother to let me take. She said it was a waste of time and insisted I should only be taking classes that would help me with my future career in accounting. But somehow, in a rare moment of weakness, or maybe just distraction, she agreed. I didn't ask twice. I do all the homework late at night when she's asleep, so she can't accuse this class of interfering with my "real" studies.

I slide into my seat just as Mrs. Rhine closes the door. She's my favorite teacher, and this class has become a kind of sanctuary for me. The one place where I can be *Sam*. And maybe even *Sammy* now too. Not the proper, always-perfect Samantha Jane my mother expects me to be.

Mrs. Rhine starts passing out last week's graded assignments, and I hold my breath, bracing myself. I might suck at math, but writing is my favorite and the one thing I know I'm good at. I poured my heart into this story, even though my mother told me to stop wasting my time on it.

My story was about a girl who dreamed of traveling the world. She went on grand adventures and tasted the freedom that comes with uncertainty. She was fearless and bold. Courageous and beautiful.

I wait, breath caught in my throat, desperate to know what Mrs. Rhine thought of it, of the life I wish I had.

Mrs. Rhine finally stops at my desk and places the paper in front of me. Circled in pink glitter pen is a single, glowing letter: A.

She leans down with a genuine smile and whispers, "Good job, Sam."

She's the only one who calls me *Sam*. And somehow, it feels like she sees something in me no one else does. *The only other person who's made me feel that way… is the new kid.*

I hold the paper up like it's a piece of treasure. Underneath the grade, in her familiar handwriting, are the words: *Don't ever stop writing, and don't ever stop dreaming. Your life and words will have an impact.*

A smile tugs at my lips, and for the first time in a while, the heaviness lifts.

Maybe my words could matter. Maybe… I could, too.

The bell rings, and I begin collecting my books, still riding the quiet high of that glowing pink A. Just as I'm about to walk out the door, Mrs. Rhine calls me over.

"Sam," she says with a warm smile, "I was very impressed by your paper. You really have a way with words."

I blush and glance down at the books in my hands, folding the corner of a page, an old nervous habit I never grew out of.

"The local college is offering a journalism course for high school students," she says. "I submitted your name. I really think it's meant for you."

My head snaps up.

She looks me directly in the eye. "You could really do this, Sam. I have full faith in you."

I stammer a thank you, my mind scrambling.

Me? A college course in journalism? That would be a dream. She really believes in me?

"Oh, Sam—wait, before you go!" she calls as I reach the door. "I almost forgot. This card was on my desk this morning. Addressed to *Sammy.* I don't have another Sam, Samantha, or Sammy besides you."

She hands me a crisp white envelope.

"I think this is for you… "

I take it cautiously, mumble another thank you, and step out into the hallway.

Who would leave me a card—and with Mrs. Rhine?

I lean against the wall. I've got a couple of minutes before my next class. Slowly, I open each corner, careful not to rip it. As the flap lifts, a scent drifts out: warm like sunshine, cool like river air, rich like wildflowers in bloom. It wraps around my mind and floods every sense. I'm shocked that something can smell so amazing, so otherworldly.

I slide out the card and unfold it.

In large gold lettering, it reads:

YOU ARE INVITED TO SEE
A GLIMPSE OF GLORY
When: Tonight
Time: Midnight
Where: Heaven

My mind goes blank. I stare at the card, stunned, then glance around to see if anyone's watching me.

Is this some kind of joke? A prank?

But who would go to the trouble, and why give it to Mrs. Rhine?

I stuff the card into the nearest trash can. It's probably nothing. Just some stupid prank.

Algebra is about to start anyway.

As soon as I walk in, all eyes fall on me.

That's when I notice: *Mr. Jones isn't here.*

My heart pounds.

The last time our teacher was late, a few of the girls thought it would be hilarious to make fun of me loudly, and in front of everyone. Whispered insults are one thing. But public humiliation? That's a whole other nightmare.

I quickly scan the room for an empty seat. Mr. Jones doesn't assign seats, but most people stick to the same spot every day. Not today. It's like they rearranged the whole room. My usual spot in the front row is taken.

"Samantha!" Megan, the leader of the mean girls, calls.

My stomach knots. *It's never a good thing when Megan gives me attention.*

I turn slowly to look at her, silently begging for Mr. Jones to walk through the door any second now.

"Why don't you come sit next to us today?" she says, smiling.

But the smile doesn't reach her eyes.

I scan the room, searching for any other seat, but realize there are none left. With no other choice, I start walking toward the one Megan offered. Behind me, the boys in the back corner start snickering.

I reach the desk, give a shaky smile, and sit down.

The room erupts with laughter.

Confused, I shift in my seat until I feel it. Something cold and damp is soaking through my clothes. I jump up, heart pounding, and look down to see a puddle of water on the chair I somehow didn't notice before. My pants are visibly drenched.

Seriously? I thought we'd moved past middle school antics.

My face turns bright red.

Megan practically shrieks with laughter. "Samantha, did you pee yourself? That's disgusting!"

More laughter erupts. A few kids have their phones out, pointed in my direction.

I stand frozen, scanning the room in panic.

The only ones who aren't laughing are the kids who get bullied too. They just shake their heads and turn away.

Jenny and Jessica laugh with the others but it's that fake, performative kind of laugh. The kind people use when they're just going along with the crowd. Too afraid to do anything. They don't even look at me.

Just as I'm about to bolt from the room, Mr. Jones finally walks in.

I nearly crash into him.

"Samantha, what happened?" he asks, concerned.

I glance back at Megan. Her glare is sharp enough to cut. I know what will happen if I say the truth. So I lie.

"I spilled some water, that's all," I mumble. "I was just going to the bathroom to dry off."

Mr. Jones narrows his eyes, looking around the classroom. He knows something's off, but he lets it go.

"Very well," he says. "Why don't you head to the nurse's office? She might have something you can change into."

I nod my thanks and hurry out of the room, down the hall toward the nurse's office, stopping just before the door to catch my breath. I need to compose myself. One look of compassion from Ms. Steele and I'll fall apart, blubbering, confessing everything.

I close my eyes and take a few deep breaths, repeating the only thought that gets me through: *This will all be over soon. None of this matters. Freedom is coming.*

Ms. Steele doesn't seem like she believes my story. I look away, hiding the tears that are starting to surface. Thankfully, she lets it go and gestures toward the lost and found.

I rummage through the box, hoping for a miracle. The only thing remotely wearable is a pair of old, musty gym shorts, not even girls' shorts. But anything's better than walking around in soaked pants all day.

I throw them on, mumble a thank you, and hurry back to class, hoping to go unnoticed.

When I walk in wearing a white button-down shirt with over-sized boys' gym shorts, the class erupts in laughter again. I keep my head down, willing myself to disappear.

Mr. Jones hushes the class and motions to a desk up front. I slip into the seat as quietly as possible.

Second and third period pass in a blur of stares, snickers, and whispered comments. I lose count of how many times I remind myself: *Just get through it. Almost done.*

Finally, it's lunchtime.

I speed-walk to the cafeteria, both desperate to eat and desperate to avoid the crowd that's clearly enjoying my humiliation today.

Lunch is the only meal my mother can't take away from me, at least not without calling the school and excusing me from lunch. Honestly, I wouldn't put it past her. She's getting worse.

My stomach growls loudly as I near the cafeteria, and I quicken my pace.

Just as I'm about to open the door, my phone vibrates in my pocket.

Odd. Who would be texting me?

I pull it out and freeze.

It's a text from Amber. Stephen's girlfriend.

> Hey Samantha, how are you? I was thinking about you today. I know it's been a long time since we've talked. Too long. I've been so busy with college and working two jobs. And missing Stephen. I'm always here if you need someone to talk to. Please respond, I'd love to hear from you.

I nearly drop my phone.

It's been over a year since I last heard from her.

Not really her fault—I stopped responding.

Shortly after Stephen died, my mother found out Amber had been texting me. She told me to cut all contact.

I tried to message Amber in secret, but my mother had access to my phone records. She knew who I was talking to. She always knew.

Amber was the last person I had left. Someone who actually knew Stephen. Someone who loved him too.

At first, she texted weekly. Then monthly. Always asking why I wasn't responding. She even called a few times… I never picked up.

She's finally reaching out again…

What if I texted back? Just once?

CHAPTER 5

*"And God saw everything that he had
made, and behold, it was very good."*

Genesis 1:31 esv

I'm rereading the text as I walk through the cafeteria doors. The smell of pizza hits me in the face, and my mouth starts watering.

"Hey, Samantha!" someone calls, but I keep walking.

"Go eat some donuts, you anorexic freak!"

The kids closest to me burst out laughing.

I had hoped that everyone seeing me eat lunch every day would put an end to the eating disorder rumors, but no such luck.

My face flushes, and I keep my head down, walking quickly past Megan and her crew.

I've tried defending myself, telling them I didn't have a disorder. But when they pushed back and asked why I was so skinny, I couldn't explain why.

If only they knew what was going on. Maybe then they wouldn't make cruel comments or laugh at me when I walk by. Maybe someone would try to help. Or maybe they'd accuse me of lying. That's more likely.

I push down the feelings of embarrassment. The words they say will stay with me all day, but as I glance back, they're deep in conversation and laughter, already having forgotten about me.

I hurry to the counter, knowing that if I'm late, the best food will be gone and I'll be stuck with the meatloaf.

I read Amber's message one more time, then delete it.

She can't help me.

I wait impatiently in line, my mouth watering with anticipation. No one here understands what it's like to eat only one meal a day. The hunger that gnaws at my stomach all day and night. I wouldn't wish it on anyone.

More kids start filing into line behind me, and suddenly, I feel something shift in the air. It feels charged. The same peace and warmth I felt this morning on the bus when the strange new kid walked on now fills the cafeteria.

Am I the only one noticing?

Everyone else continues their business like nothing's happening.

I cautiously glance toward the door. Joshua is standing there, scanning the room, just as I knew he would be. I start to turn away quickly, not wanting to be caught looking, but his eyes meet mine. He smiles. That infectious smile lights up his whole face. I suddenly feel even more unsure of myself.

He waves and I wave back without thinking.

In his hand, I notice he's holding a book and it looks like the one from the bus. My face heats up, turning crimson. *Why does he carry that thing with him everywhere? Who just walks around holding a Bible unless they're a preacher… or some religious nut?*

I hate people who rub their righteousness in everyone's face. That's not someone I want to be associated with.

I quickly face forward in line, thankful it's long enough that I won't have to stand next to him.

But just when I think I'm in the clear, I hear a cheerful voice right beside me.

"Hey! What's up, Sammy?"

Somehow, my face turns even redder. Kids in line start snickering and tossing comments under their breath.

Anger starts bubbling up. *We only met this morning. Why is he embarrassing me like this? I can't just ignore him, though. That would only make things even more awkward.*

"Oh, hey Joshua. Just grabbing some lunch… "

Joshua chuckles, completely unfazed by the stares and snickering happening right next to us. His eyes flick briefly to my outfit, but he graciously says nothing and keeps talking. For that, I'm thankful.

"Sorry to bug you, I was just wondering if you'd want to eat outside with me. It's too nice of a day to stay cooped up in here."

I shuffle forward as the line moves, Joshua keeping pace beside me.

Normally, I eat lunch in the library. The librarian took pity on me after finding me eating in the girls' bathroom one day. There was no one to sit with in the cafeteria. And eating in the bathroom wasn't that bad… but the library was better.

I glance anxiously at the lunch monitors. They're huddled together at a table in the corner, faces buried in their phones. *Maybe we won't get caught.* A few kids sneak outside sometimes, but I've never been one of them. I can't take the risk. Getting in trouble at school means dealing with something far worse at home.

All those thoughts swirl in my head, but what comes out of my mouth surprises even me.

"Sure."

Joshua smiles. "Cool," he says, then walks away.

He's new here, but he doesn't seem fazed. He walks with his head high, his steps slow and confident.

The lunch lady clears her throat, clearly impatient.

I mumble, "Sorry," grab two slices of pepperoni pizza, pay the grumpy lunch lady, and glance around for Joshua.

I find him leaning casually against the cafeteria door that leads outside, his face tilted toward the ceiling, eyes closed, a small smile tugging at the corners of his mouth.

This kid is even stranger than I thought.

I walk up and stop in front of Joshua. He hasn't noticed me yet.

For a moment, I just watch him, stunned by the peace on his face.

Just below his hairline, I spot a jagged scar. It must have been hidden earlier on the bus, only becoming visible now with his head tilted back.

I wonder how he got it.

My eyes drift down to his, and to my shock, they're open. For what feels like the millionth time today, my face flushes red.

He looks at me, and I'm confused to see tears in his eyes. But not tears of sadness, something else.

I quickly look away. "Sorry for staring… you just looked really peaceful. I didn't want to bother you."

Nice cover-up, Samantha.

"Is everything alright?"

He clears his throat, chuckling nervously. "Yeah, everything's great, Sammy."

He grabs my arm and pulls me toward the door. "Come on, before the lunch monitor sees us."

We slip out the door and the sun pours onto my face. A gentle breeze blows a strand of hair that's worked itself free. *There's nothing like a spring day in Maine.*

Before I realize what's happening, Joshua takes off running across the yard.

"Come on, Sammy!" he calls.

He looks so free and happy that I can't help myself. I run too, laughing at how ridiculous it is.

For a moment, I feel like a carefree kid again.

What's happening to me?

Joshua beats me to the end of the yard, but I arrive shortly after, clutching my pizza like it's a baby.

He stops at the edge of the woods and stares intently into the dark brush. It's Maine; there are trees everywhere, but Joshua looks into the forest like it's the first time he's ever seen trees.

"Check out this pine! It's massive. Okay, sure, compared to the redwoods it's tiny; but still, pretty impressive. I'm officially claiming it as my spot."

We make our way to the pine. It's bigger than I expected, its wide branches offering the perfect place to sit and hide from the world.

We plop down next to the tree and start eating in silence. The sunshine warms my skin. The quiet company, odd as it is, feels strangely comforting. It's been two years since I've sat with someone without feeling sick to my stomach or burning with embarrassment as they ignored me, or worse, made fun of me.

Joshua points things out from time to time: a cloud that looks like a bunny, then an actual bunny that hops across the yard. I'm used to all the wildlife, but Joshua is amused by it like it's the first time he's ever seen nature. I glance at the cloud again. If I tilt my head just right, I guess I can see a bunny. But every time Joshua looks at it, he laughs like he's in on some inside joke with the sky.

"I can't get enough of nature. Every time I stop and really look, I'm blown away. Take clouds, for instance, how cool are they? God really knew what he was doing when he made all this."

There it is again, that God talk.

I've never met anyone who talks about God so casually, like he's just a normal part of everyday conversation. It bothers me more than I'd like to admit. I don't believe in some big guy in the sky who sends people to hell. But still, every time Joshua brings him up, something in my chest tightens. It aches, like I'm missing something I used to have but forgot.

I drift into thought, but every once in a while I catch Joshua smiling at me. It makes me blush. I feel like he can see straight through me and I hate that. I don't want anyone to know the truth about me.

After sitting in silence for a while, Joshua speaks first.

"Sammy, can I ask you a question?"

Whenever someone asks that question, it's never something good. But I had already gone along with his other odd requests, so why not one more?

"Sure, Joshua. What is it?"

Joshua turns so he's facing me.

"I know it's kind of personal, especially since we just met this morning, but… what makes you happy?"

I'm caught off guard by the question and too stunned to answer. I stammer out the very intelligent phrase, "I don't know."

Joshua doesn't let it slide that easily.

He gestures to everything around us.

"Come on. We live in this amazing world, there's got to be something that makes you happy. I just want to get to know you better."

I look around, trying to see what he sees. The trees are the same ones I've known my entire life. The sky is blue, the sun is bright. It's all the same. Nothing special.

Still, I force myself to meet his eyes, so full of joy.

I feel myself relax.

And then, out of nowhere, a thought slips in. *Nighttime.*

Before I can stop it, I blurt it out.

"Nighttime."

Joshua nods slowly, encouraging me to continue.

"When I was a kid, my dad used to take me and my brother outside on clear nights to look at the stars. Every time we spotted a shooting star, he'd tell us to make a wish. It felt so… magical. That's when I fell in love with nighttime. Even now, when the sky starts to darken and I see that first star, I feel happy, even if it's just for a moment."

I quickly look away from Joshua's warm eyes, which are now glowing even brighter after hearing my story. I start plucking blades of grass from the dirt, shocked that I just shared one of my most precious memories with someone I barely know.

"Wow, Sammy. That's really beautiful." Joshua's voice softens. "I hope I didn't push you too hard. I really appreciate you sharing that with me."

He pauses, then gently asks, "Does your brother go to school too?"

The familiar pain tightens in my chest. It's been a while since I've met someone who hasn't heard about the accident. I could lie. He wouldn't know any different, and it's not like I'm going to be around for long. *So what does it matter?*

But something about Joshua makes me want to tell the truth.

"My brother died two years ago." It's all I can manage to get out.

Joshua, seeing the tears forming in my eyes, doesn't push for more. Instead, he gently reaches over and squeezes my hand, offering a sad smile.

Then, like it's the most natural thing in the world, he lays back on the grass, sticks a piece of straw between his teeth like he's in an old Western, and closes his eyes. I'm stunned.

How did he get me to open up so easily? And where on earth did he even find a piece of straw?

He's the strangest boy I have ever met. Carefree. Full of contentment and joy. He embraces life in a way I can't understand. And I want whatever it is he has.

Earth to Samantha. Pull it together.

Just because I made a friend today doesn't mean life is magically better. Once my mother finds out about Joshua, it'll be over.

She's determined for me to succeed, either by my own strength or by marrying into it. And it's clear Joshua doesn't come from wealth. Holes in his jeans. A stain on his shirt. To my mother, that's all she'll need to disapprove.

With that painful reminder, I jump to my feet. Joshua looks confused and shoots up.

"I gotta go, Joshua. I have to study for a test next period."

I walk away without looking back.

Joshua has been a good friend for today. But if he really knew me… if he knew the truth, he wouldn't want to be my friend. So what's the point? I'm not sticking around long enough for any of this to matter.

CHAPTER 6

"In the beginning, God created the heavens and the earth."

GENESIS 1:1 ESV

I quietly close my door and change into some worn but comfy pajamas. Sitting down at my vanity, I start the painstaking process of taking my hair down. My scalp is screaming from the tight bun. Running a comb through my hair, I stare into the mirror. Staring back at me: flat, lifeless eyes, pale skin dotted with too many freckles, and thin, dying hair.

It's been an emotionally charged day: the college course offer, that strange invitation, the bullying, and my unexpected conversations with Joshua. It's all too much to process.

Coming home didn't make things easier.

I found my mother on the couch, wrapped in her faded bathrobe, hair unbrushed, eyes glazed over as the daily news played on mute.

She didn't even flinch when I walked in, just gave me a brief glance and motioned for me to go upstairs.

I've never understood why I have to look perfect when she rarely even gets dressed anymore.

Anger and frustration billow inside me until numbness comes to take their place.

Lord, help me.

The words slip out before I can stop them.

The last time I prayed for help was in the hospital room, the night Stephen and I got into the car accident.

I prayed for God to switch us out. Take me instead of Stephen.

He didn't answer.

Stephen died. And my parents blamed me.

I blamed myself too.

I don't even know why I'm bothering now.

God isn't real.

He never helps me, not when I need it most.

So why would he help me now?

That's why I have to take matters into my own hands.

I'm going to make things right.

Stephen wasn't supposed to die that night. I was.

I make my way to the bed and flop down. As I lay staring at the ceiling, I think about the good times and smile a sad smile, knowing it's almost over.

The pain will end soon.

It's 11 by the time I settle down enough to sleep.

My eyes are red and aching from crying.

I'm almost there.

I drift into a restless sleep.

* * *

My room is completely dark. I squint, trying to get my eyes to adjust. I don't know what time it is, but something woke me up.

I glance at the clock. It's midnight, which means I've only been asleep for less than an hour. I groan and throw my blanket over my face. A light starts to filter through my blanket like the first rays of morning light. Confused, I remove my blanket.

My eyes widen and my jaw drops. Standing at the end of my bed is a glowing figure, draped in long white robes that flow gracefully, as if stirred by a gentle breeze.

As the light softens, I'm finally able to look straight at it. *It's a woman.*

"Sammy," Her singsong voice startles me. It carries the sound of a hundred accents, blended into something I've never heard before.

I reach for my phone, fear coursing through my veins. I need to call for help.

"Do not be afraid," she says gently. "You did receive the invitation, right? Why are you startled, Sammy? It did say midnight. Am I early?"

She glances at the clock on my nightstand, a gesture that makes her seem almost human.

I grip my phone tightly and squeeze my eyes shut, trying to convince myself this is just some kind of vivid, weird dream.

This isn't real. This isn't real.

I slowly peek through my eyelids.

She's still standing there, one eyebrow raised and a smirk playing on her lips.

Her long, curly hair cascades down to her waist, wild and untamed.

Striking emerald eyes draw me in. I stare into them, unable to look away.

"Who are you?" is all I can manage to say.

She smiles softly.

"I'm an angel. Who else would be bringing you to Heaven?"

My mind flashes back to the invitation I found earlier, the one that had mysteriously appeared in Mrs. Rhine's classroom.

"Oh… I see. You didn't believe the invite was real?" She laughs gently. "I do this so often, I sometimes forget how unbelievable it might seem. No worries, my dear. Get dressed and come with me."

She hands me a flowing, soft pink blouse and a pair of denim jeans. It's simple, but somehow perfect.

"This color looks beautiful on you," she says with a smile. "It makes your eyes pop. They shine bright, just like you."

I take the clothes, stunned in every way.

I need to snap out of this. This is too weird. Too impossible.

But I don't move. I just stand there, frozen.

What is happening?

"What am I supposed to do?" I ask, my voice barely above a whisper.

She stays calm, completely unfazed by my confusion.

"Just take my hand. Trust me."

I look into her eyes, and the fear begins to melt away.

Deep down, I know I can trust her.

"There is someone who needs you to see a glimpse of glory."

My legs feel like stone. Yet somehow, I step forward.

I reach for her hand and the moment our skin touches, everything changes.

My pajamas vanish, replaced by the soft pink blouse and denim jeans.

They fit perfectly, and for the first time in a long while, I feel like me.

And then we're shooting upward.

I brace myself, expecting to slam into the ceiling. *What is she thinking?*

But before we reach it… we're gone.

Frantically looking around, I realize we're traveling through some kind of tunnel, bright and colorful light spiraling all around us.

I'm still holding the angel's hand, afraid that if I let go, I'll fall.

My body feels weightless as we soar. I don't know how long we've been here, time seems to drift away, like it no longer exists. And honestly, it doesn't matter. There's a quiet peace settling in my chest, like I could stay here forever.

We continue speeding through this tunnel of light, my brain scrambling to comprehend what's happening.

Is this space? A different dimension? Am I hallucinating?

The farther we go, the more my senses awaken.

I can see, hear, taste, smell, and feel a multitude of sensations all at once.

It's like my soul is breathing for the first time.

We come to the end of it, and my feet land on solid ground.

Gold ground.

The angel announces, "Here we are, Sammy. Welcome to Heaven."

I was expecting to be floating among the clouds, angels singing Sunday School songs before a God on a throne, demanding everyone to bow at his feet.

What I see before me is not that.

It's a city, but not like New York City.

It's the kind of city you read about in fairytale books set in far-away lands.

A city where a princess lives and waits for her Prince Charming.

A city where nothing bad ever happens.

I'm blown away by the richness of gold in everything I see. In the roads. The buildings. Shimmering in the light, giving the illusion it's moving.

Every surface glimmers with bright red rubies and green emeralds, forming intricate designs and artwork woven into the streets and buildings for everyone to admire.

The light catches the emeralds, scattering shades of green that shimmer like a rainbow across the streets.

What really catches my attention, though, are the people.

There are men, women, and children of all different ages and ethnicities, all living together in what looks like a peaceful, close-knit community.

Each man is entirely unique, but all share similar traits: strong, noble, and moving with purpose.

The women radiate beauty, courage, and joy, carrying themselves with strength and grace that lights up everything around them.

The children run around laughing and playing, not a single one left alone.

The air hums with conversation and joy. People are working, playing, resting—together.

Whatever this is… I want it.

An aroma of spices fills the air, blending in perfect harmony, swirling around me with the rich scents of every nationality.

I follow the smell and spot a group of men, women, and children cooking side by side.

A long table is set before them, and one by one, they bring their creations for everyone to taste.

There's laughter and celebration, voices filled with joy as they praise each other for what they've made.

A smile spreads across my face as I watch them.

I look around and notice others tucked off to the side, noses deep in books, flipping pages with what seems like superhuman speed, soaking in every word.

They sit together in peaceful silence, content just to be near one another.

Elsewhere, some are reading aloud, sharing what they've learned as if they were great philosophers, their voices loud and passionate.

I wonder if there are writers here—authors, journalists. That's where you would find me.

There is so much happening all at once, I can barely take it in.

The angel woman who brought me here watches my wide-eyed expression and laughs.

"It's breathtaking, isn't it?" she says. "Watching people live out the passions God gave them, together, in community."

I look at her again, still trying to grasp what I'm seeing.

"This is so beautiful," I say, "but I don't understand. Where's God? Where are all the angels? Where are the clouds?"

She laughs again and it's the most whimsical sound I've ever heard.

I could listen to an angel laugh all day.

"Humans have always tried to guess what Heaven would be like," she says, her eyes twinkling.

"Unfortunately, their limited belief only allowed them to picture clouds. Such a shame. This is just the beginning of what you will see. Come, let's walk the city together. There's so much waiting for you."

Her eyes sparkle, and I laugh, feeling a little embarrassed that I'm one of those humans who pictured Heaven as just a pile of clouds.

It dawns on me suddenly: *if Heaven is real, that means God is real too.*

Well… where is he? Why can't I see him?

Maybe this is just the afterlife. If you do good, you get to go to this cool city.

Or maybe I'm just dreaming.

If I am dreaming, then I'm going to enjoy this.

This is way better than real life, and I'll stay here for as long as I can.

We start walking through the golden city. Warmth and peace surround me.

Immediately, I think of Joshua.

Isn't this the same feeling I felt when he was near?

That's… strange.

As we walk, the people stop what they're doing and look up, noticing me.

Immediately, my insecurities rise. I look down, afraid to meet their eyes.

Oh no. Here come the whispers.

But there aren't any whispers.

Instead, one by one, they approach me.

I feel a nudge from the angel and cautiously look up. A woman stands in front of me, her eyes crinkling with delight as she smiles. She takes my hands gently in hers.

"We are so glad you're here."

She gives them a soft squeeze, then walks away. I watch her as she joins a group of women nearby. She says something to them, and they all turn to look at me, smiling, waving.

I slowly wave back, feeling a swirl of emotions.

Are they making fun of me?

Before I can figure it out, a man walks up to me. I tense, glancing at the angel for reassurance.

She offers an encouraging smile, and I feel safe.

"Hello!" His voice is deep and welcoming. I let myself relax, just a little.

"Welcome. We are so happy to have you visit us."

Then, his expression shifts, grows serious, and I tense again.

"You are worth more than rubies and emeralds," he says. "I hope you'll see how beautiful, how special, and how loved you truly are."

I look into his eyes.

They remind me of my father's.

Tears threaten, but I push them down and give him a small nod, eyes dropping to the ground.

Then, a little girl walks up and takes my hand.

She looks up into the face I'm trying to hide.

She looks just like I did when I was little with a big, innocent smile and brown hair sticking up in every direction.

"You're pretty," she says, with the purest eyes I've ever seen.

She giggles and runs off to join her friends.

I let out a small chuckle.

One by one, others come to welcome me.

Each one tells me how precious and loved I am, that I'm full of spunk and creativity.

I can't believe what I'm seeing or hearing. My eyes sting with tears as I let the words I've so desperately needed to hear wash over me.

The angel woman places her hand on my shoulder, gives me a look of knowing, and whispers, "You are seen here, Sammy."

Such simple words, yet they strike me to my core.

I am seen.

We continue our walk through the streets.

A gentle breeze stirs the air, and with it, an overwhelming peace fills my body from head to toe.

Beneath my feet, the walkway shifts into smooth cobblestone.

I trail my fingers along the golden buildings, brushing the green vines that snake up their sides.

It all feels enchanted, like the city itself is inviting you to explore, to wander without destination or end.

Along the path, we stop to admire a man carving the most

incredible toys from beechwood: boats, planes, and an assortment of other creations.

He carves each one from a block of wood with such precision, it's mesmerizing to watch.

Fueled by his love for the craft, he gazes at every finished toy with admiration before moving on to the next. Little children surround him, taking turns playing with the toys. The man generously hands them out, and the children squeal with joy.

He takes his time with each creation, pouring all of himself into it, finding complete satisfaction in the process.

This is what he loves to do. And he enjoys every moment of it.

He looks up, and across from him approaches a woman with long brown hair and a radiant smile. They meet in an embrace like best friends. She playfully grabs the new toy he's working on and starts carving. I hear her whisper that she is the faster of the two. The man chuckles and they work side by side, sharing easy conversation and enjoying each other's company.

And that's how everyone is.

There is no one alone.

We walk a little farther and stop to watch a woman creating exquisite clothing.

She works the machine with ease and confidence, producing silk gowns that would rival anything from a Hollywood designer.

Other women line up to admire her work, and when she finishes one, she passes it to one of them. They all delight in the clothing. Some put on the dresses and twirl around, dancing and laughing.

Everyone seems so happy.

I'm baffled by everything I see. It's nothing like I thought Heaven was supposed to be.

"Excuse me, um… um…" I stammer, feeling pathetic.

She smiles gently, not the least bit fazed.

"You can call me Marie."

Marie.

That's a perfect name for an angel.

"Marie, I'm sorry, but I don't understand any of this. I didn't expect Heaven to be like this. I didn't even believe it was real! Why is everyone still working? And just… living normal lives? Doesn't that all end when we die?"

I spin around, taking it all in.

"How can this be Heaven?"

Marie takes me by the hand to a dark oak bench with carvings of lions on the ends of the armrests. Down the legs, intricate rosebuds and vines twist and wrap around.

I wonder if the toy makers made this too.

The bench sits in a vast garden at the center of the city. Rose bushes bloom all around us, and wildflowers are scattered with careful intention.

There's not a patch of ground that isn't bursting with color.

I find the source of the flowers: men, women, and children kneeling in the rich soil spread throughout the garden.

They are planting, seed by seed, into the fertile ground. Each time they gently cover a seed, water springs up from the earth, soaking the soil and causing a flower to burst into magnificent color.

Joy spreads across their faces, a fresh wave of wonder with every new blossom.

They never grow tired of it. Each bloom is celebrated.

The smell is heavenly—no pun intended.

I chuckle to myself, and Marie looks down at me with a smirk on her face, as if she can read my mind and hear my terrible jokes.

"Sammy, I don't have all the answers you're searching for. One day, God called me to him and assigned me to you. He said it was time to bring you to Heaven."

She pauses, her voice softens.

"He's inviting you to explore, to see for yourself the glory that awaits all his children."

Dumbfounded by her words, I sit in complete shock and silence. A million thoughts swirl in my mind.

Am I going to see God? I need to know.

"Marie, do I get to see God? Isn't he the whole point of Heaven?"

She places her arm around my shoulder in a motherly way, and I sink into her embrace, trying to remember the last time I had been hugged by my own mother.

"You will see him, but only when the story is finished and all things are restored. But now is not the time. Let's keep venturing on. Write down all that you see. God wants to see it from your perspective."

What story is she talking about? And how am I supposed to write anything down?

"Write? But how can I without…"

My words trail off as I look down and find, resting in my lap, a handcrafted leather-bound journal engraved with the words:

To my beloved, your journey awaits you.

Those words soften my heart.

I am someone's beloved?

I look up at Marie, tears misting my eyes. She wraps both arms around me, and I lean into her, letting myself feel loved and comforted.

We sit there for a moment, listening to the breeze blow through the garden and the birds chirping in the distance, singing a song to one another.

I wish I could stay here forever.

I glance around, taking in all the grandeur, when I notice something unusual.

Doors.

Placed randomly.

On the street. In the garden. Everywhere.

They stand on their own, unattached to any building.

Above each one hangs a sign with a name: *"Cappadocia," "Whitsundays," "Isle of Skye," "Grand Canyon," "Huacachina."*

I recognize these names because I've spent half my life daydreaming about travel.

Cappadocia is in Turkey, known for its strange but beautiful landscape. I've always dreamed of flying in one of their famous hot air balloons. The Whitsundays are in Australia, the Isle of Skye is in Scotland, the Grand Canyon is in the U.S., and Huacachina is in Peru.

These are the exact places I've always dreamed of visiting.

As I keep scanning, I see hundreds upon hundreds more scattered about, each marked with a different name.

I look up at Marie, who is watching me like a mother on Christmas morning, smiling, encouraging me to take a closer look.

"Sammy, this is a journey you need to take on your own. Go explore. There's someone very excited to meet you."

I hug her and thank her for bringing me here.

With a tearful goodbye, unsure of what to do next, I walk slowly toward the door that glows softly in the distance. It draws me in.

Cappadocia.

My heart is pounding with anticipation.

All I know is that on the other side of this door is the beginning. And for a rare moment, I feel hopeful.

I'm ready to see a glimpse of glory.

CHAPTER 7

*"For God so loved the world, that he gave his only
Son, that whoever believes in him should not perish
but have eternal life. For God did not send his Son
into the world to condemn the world, but in order
that the world might be saved through him."*

JOHN 3:16-17 ESV

Feeling a sudden surge of boldness, I reach for the doorknob.

Slowly turning it, I push the door open.

Please don't let this all be a joke.

I'm not sure what I'm expecting, maybe a tiger to jump out and startle me awake from this dream?

Instead, what my eyes fall upon takes my breath away.

Wow. This is unbelievable.

The landscape shifts before me.

No longer cautious, I step through.

Tall, cone-shaped rock formations stretch toward the bright blue sky.

I'm transported to a magical land dotted with colorful hot air balloons, drifting high above the jagged terrain like leaves in autumn air.

To the west, I spot a city built into the rocks, white stone buildings seamlessly woven into the earth.

From above, you might not even notice it's there.

The glow of lanterns scattered throughout gives it a haunting beauty.

Reading about this back home couldn't have prepared me for what I'm seeing now.

I remember my journal and sit down in a shady spot beside a rock. A cool breeze washes over me as I begin to write.

> Cappadocia, known for its "fairy chimneys" in central Turkey, is even more beautiful than I imagined. I feel like I've stumbled onto a secret, as if I've been invited to witness a nearly hidden city. If it weren't for the hot air balloons, you might not even know it's here. There's a ruby-red balloon with yellow zigzag patterns. That one's my favorite. Every color is accounted for; there's even a rainbow one so vivid it practically glows against the clear blue sky. Every so often, one dips low, and I hold my breath, waiting for it to scrape the fairy chimneys, but then the roar of its flame lifts it gently back up.

I'm so engrossed in my writing, I don't notice the man by the river to the east.

When I finally look up, I see him leaning against a tree at the river's edge, watching the balloons and smiling with delight.

He must have felt my gaze, because he turns and our eyes meet.

A smile spreads across his face, and I'm struck by the beauty of it.

He pushes off the tree and calls out, "Sammy! Come on down to the river!"

How does this man know me?

I'm drawn to him, and my feet start moving before my mind can catch up, a common theme in this dream. I'm being pulled by an unseen force, and I have no desire to fight it.

The closer I get, the more my heart fills with unexplainable peace and joy.

This can't be…

My brain is telling me it's impossible, but I know who this is.

I know immediately the closer I get.

My heart remembers him from Sunday School stories.

There was a time I knew this man and believed in him. A time when I was just a child, with faith that could move mountains.

I walk slowly. He remains by the tree, patiently waiting.

Then, I run.

I run as fast as I can. Just before I reach him, I stumble, but he catches me.

I wrap my arms around his waist and start weeping.

"Jesus," I whisper through sobs. "Is it really you?"

He holds me, gently stroking my hair. I feel warm tears fall onto my head.

Is he crying too?

I pull back and look into his eyes. They are gentle and kind. Tears run unashamedly down his face.

He smiles at me, and for a moment all my troubles melt away.

"My precious friend," he says, "it's so good to see you. How are you?"

I cry harder, unable to explain the pain that I feel.

Jesus hugs me tighter.

"I'm so sorry, Sammy. I'm sorry for all the pain you've had to go through. I've longed to take it away. From the moment you were born, I had a plan for your life. The enemy saw how precious you are to me and he's been trying to destroy it ever since."

He gently wipes the tears falling from my eyes.

"But when the enemy thinks all is destroyed and lost," he says softly, "I bring beauty out of ashes."

He points toward the regal hot air balloons rising from the rugged ground into the bright blue sky, defying gravity.

"And that's exactly what I have planned for you. I came to earth and died so you could be free. Free from pain, from shame."

He looks at me with love shining in his eyes.

"You are precious to me, my dear Samantha Jane. Every tear you cry, I see. Every single drop is collected in a bottle. I love you with all my heart."

The walls around my heart begin to lower. I let the soothing balm of his words wash over me, healing the shattered pieces of my soul. Hearing my full name spoken in love—instead of the harsh way my mother uses it—makes me feel seen. Known. Loved for who I truly am.

All I had learned about him from my early days back when we used to go to church comes rushing back to memory. I used to believe he existed, but that faith left me a long time ago.

Standing here in Jesus' embrace, I want to believe again, but I'm struggling.

If Jesus truly loves me, why didn't he stop my life from falling apart?

The questions swirl in my mind, too heavy to hold in, but I'm scared to let them out.

He doesn't flinch.

"I'm not afraid of your questions, Sammy. You can ask them."

I hesitate for just a moment, then I blurt it all out.

All my anger, fears, and frustrations come pouring out in a flood.

"I prayed. I asked you to save Stephen! But you didn't! I even offered myself in his place, but you didn't listen! Now my mother hates me. Why? And why doesn't my father love me anymore? How can I believe you love me when I've lost everyone I've ever loved? I'm completely alone!"

My body shakes uncontrollably.

For a moment, I'm afraid I've gone too far.

Maybe he didn't really mean it when he said I could ask anything.

Will he punish me now?

Tears fall from his eyes, his face stricken with grief.

He touches my arm, and suddenly, all the anger and pain leave my body.

His body begins to contort, agony twisting across his face.

He holds out his arms palms upward, and I watch in horror, unable to understand what's happening.

My eyes drift from his face to his hands.

There, on his palms, I see the remnants of what he did on the cross.

The holes are healed, but they remain.

A stark reminder of what he endured.

From his hands, a black mist rises into the sky.

Inside it, I hear my own cries from just moments ago.

As it rises, the mist shifts from black to red, then from red to white until it disappears completely.

In its place, peace settles over me.

I look back into Jesus' eyes, searching for an answer to what I just witnessed.

They are clear and bright.

No pain remains on his face.

Jesus leads me back to the tree near the river and sits down, patting the ground next to him for me to join.

He begins to explain, "Every cry, every prayer, whether whispered intentionally or unintentionally, I take and bring to my Father on your behalf. Not one has gone unheard. Your questions are valid. Your anger is too. I can handle it, Sammy."

He looks out over the grand landscape and sighs.

"Eden was beautiful. You were meant to live side by side with us. But everything changed when Adam and Eve ate the fruit that gave them the knowledge of good and evil. They used their free will, the very gift my Father gave all humanity, to disobey the one command that would have protected them from ever knowing shame, sadness, or loneliness."

I think back to the story of Adam and Eve.

I never understood then that God was protecting them, not withholding anything good from them.

Maybe there's more I've been wrong about.

Jesus takes my hand and gives it a reassuring squeeze.

"That's when pain entered the world. A pain that was never supposed to exist. But my Father, in his unrelenting kindness, has been fighting for his creation ever since. He's never stopped pursuing the ones he loves."

He turns to me, eyes full of both sorrow and hope.

"But you see, a pattern kept emerging: when life was good, people forgot about God, the one who created them, the one who loved them. They chose their own desires over a relationship with their Creator. But the moment they were in trouble, they cried out for help and he came. Again and again, the cycle repeated."

His eyes fill with tears once more. My heart aches seeing them.

"If he removed free will, everyone would choose him, but it wouldn't be love. It wouldn't be a real relationship. And that's what he longs for, Sammy. He created humanity to walk with them. To be their Father. Their friend. To show them the beauty and goodness of life. In this world, you will have trouble. But I have overcome the world. Bad things will continue to happen until my Father says it's time to return and restore everything. To make everything as it was always meant to be."

I'm mesmerized by every word, my brain scrambling to fully comprehend.

"Even now, he is still fighting for every heart that hasn't yet discovered his love and goodness. As long as free will exists on earth, pain will remain. People make their own choices. But hear this, Sammy: for those who believe in me, we are working all things together for their good. We will bring beauty from the ashes. There is hope beyond your world."

Tears flow freely from my eyes as I listen, hearing about how deeply God loves all that he created.

I still don't fully understand it, but I feel ashamed that I turned my back on him when things got hard.

I stopped believing, just as Jesus described.

I look away, unable to meet the gaze of the one sent to save us all.

He speaks gently, "Sammy, I took that shame on the cross. There's no need to look away. Look at me, and receive the gift I'm handing to you."

I look up, half expecting him to be holding an actual gift.

But what I see in his eyes is better: *grace. hope. love. freedom.*

Everything I've been longing for being offered freely in this very moment.

It's here for the taking.

Come on, Sammy. This is real. He is real.

"I believe," is all I manage to squeak out.

He smiles and in an instant that smile melts away all my fears, flooding me with joy.

Laughter bubbles up from deep inside me. I have no control over it.

I roll onto the ground, clutching my stomach, feeling unabashedly free.

Jesus laughs too. His laughter is bold, echoing through the canyons like music.

We sit there laughing for a long time, just enjoying the moment.

I finally get a hold of myself, wiping away the tears of joy from my eyes.

I look at Jesus, my Savior.

He is beautiful.

Glory radiates from him, and I am in awe.

How could I have forgotten him?

No longer afraid to talk, I speak freely.

"Is this where you live in Heaven? In Turkey? I thought you were supposed to be on the throne?"

Jesus smiles and looks around.

People from the city have noticed him by the river and wave gleefully, but they don't flock around him like I expected.

I'd spend every moment with him if I could.

But even though they look at him with awe and wonder, they keep their distance and continue what they're doing.

He turns back to me.

"Well, Sammy... yes, I live here because it's where your heart wanted to go. But I also live in every corner of the world, and now again in your heart. In the heart of everyone who believes. I live everywhere."

That leaves me with even more questions.

Jesus can clearly read my thoughts because he starts into further detail.

"I am in all things. I know it's hard to grasp, but just as I am here with you, I am also in the city with them, just in different ways. There is no time here, and because of that, I can be everywhere at once. I've said before that not everything about me can be fully understood, and even here, with everything at your fingertips, this is one mystery that may never make complete sense."

He squeezes my hand and I nod.

It makes sense in my heart, even if my mind still struggles to catch up.

I rest my head on his shoulder and close my eyes.

Peace washes over me.

We sit there for what feels like an eternity—maybe it has been that long.

I can't tell.

Finally, Jesus speaks.

"Are you ready to see the next place?"

"The next place?" I ask, lifting my head.

Jesus chuckles. "Of course. Why stay in one place when there's so much more to see? Come with me. I want to travel with you."

At this point, if this is all a dream, then it's the wildest, most amazing dream I've ever had.

Suddenly, before us, another door appears.

Over it is a sign that reads: *Whitsundays Island.*

My heart starts beating with anticipation once again.

Jesus looks down at me with a twinkle in his eye.

"Are you ready?"

CHAPTER 8

"But, as it is written, "What no eye has seen, nor
ear heard, nor the heart of man imagined, what
God has prepared for those who love him."

1 CORINTHIANS 2:9 ESV

We step through the door, but instead of solid ground beneath us, a warm liquid envelops me from head to toe.

I instinctively shut my eyes.

Gasping, my arms flail as I try to make sense of what's happening. When I finally open them, I'm surprised to find myself treading in warm, crystal-clear, calm water.

This must be the Coral Sea.

I look around in shock. When it said Whitsundays Island, I wasn't expecting to be dropped into the ocean. In the distance, I spot the island with its pristine white beaches glistening under the sun.

I let out a laugh as I realize I'm effortlessly floating.

Curiosity takes over and I dive beneath the surface, suddenly consumed with the desire to go deeper.

I take a risk and open my eyes underwater. Expecting the sting of saltwater, I squeeze them shut again, but the sting never comes.

To my amazement, I can see clearly, just as if I were still above the water.

Wow, this is incredible.

Despite not being a strong swimmer, I glide through the water, my feet moving as if I'm wearing invisible flippers. For a moment, I panic. Surely, I've been under too long. Any second now, I'll run out of air.

But the moment never comes.

I feel like a mermaid. Five-year-old Sammy would be ecstatic! Her dream finally came true.

I finally feel the need for fresh, salty air, so I push my way to the surface.

Taking a deep breath, I dive under again.

This time, I see it, what I've dreamed of my whole life: the Great Barrier Reef.

My eyes take in every color of fish one could imagine: deep blues, fiery oranges, shimmering greens, yellows as bright as the sun. They all swim below the surface, casting rainbows of color in the sunlight. My heart jumps when I see sharks swarming around me, hammerheads, tiger sharks, and even wobbegongs, but they pay no attention to me.

I'm tempted to reach out and touch one, but stop myself.

Then again, this could be a dream… or it could really be Heaven. Anything feels possible here.

I extend my arm toward a tiger shark slowly drifting by and touch its fin. Electricity shoots through my body, and I feel fully alive.

Suddenly, it gets very dark.

A shadow blocks the sunlight from reaching me below the surface.

I look up, expecting a giant shark, but to my surprise, it's a fever of stingrays gliding majestically above me.

I reach up and let my fingertips trail along the magnificent creatures, no longer afraid.

I propel myself back up to the surface and let out a joyous whoop.

I'm swimming in the Coral Sea along the Great Barrier Reef!

I thought the hot air balloons were amazing, but this… this is unreal.

I keep swimming, exploring the reef, discovering all kinds of treasures hidden below the surface.

But then it hits me.

Where's Jesus?

I've been so caught up in the wonder of it all, I didn't even notice he wasn't beside me anymore.

Panic sets in.

I glance around frantically.

Where is he?

The water starts to feel warmer and begins to swirl around me, shimmering gold and varying shades of blue. I look up, trying to make sense of it.

An ear-splitting grin spreads across my face.

Of course. It's him.

Jesus is sailing toward me, steering a boat with two massive sails, bright white, billowing in the coastal breeze.

The wind dies and the sailboat drifts to a gentle stop beside me.

Still bobbing in the warm water, I see a hand reach down.

I grab it, and in one smooth motion, I'm hoisted onto a teak deck, sturdy and warm beneath my feet.

I glance up at the towering mast, shielding my eyes from the sun as glints of gold and turquoise catch my gaze, woven into the trim of the sail.

It glimmers in the light like something out of a dream.

Sea creatures are carved into the bow of the boat, and as the waves move beneath us, they give the illusion of leaping in and out of the water.

Jesus greets me with his infectious smile, and I can't help but return it.

We stand in silence for a while, gazing out across the Coral Sea off Whitsunday Island.

The water shifts from aqua blue to emerald green, blending together in a mesmerizing swirl, shimmering flecks of gold dancing across the surface.

I'm amazed I'm here—with Jesus.

My friend?

Jesus's smile widens and he pulls me into a warm hug.

Yep. Definitely reading my mind.

"How was your swim?" he asks, just before dashing to the sails as the wind suddenly picks up.

I barely brace myself in time before the wind fills the canvas, launching us forward.

Jesus glances back at me with a playful wink.

"Hold on tight!"

Slicing through, we pave a path for the dolphins to follow in our wake.

I laugh as the water sprays my face, forgetting that Jesus asked me a question.

I hold my hand out to touch the water, and a curious bottlenose dolphin joins my fingertips.

It leaps in the air, splashing me and the boat.

Laughter spills from my mouth as I look up at Jesus, who is busy manning the sails.

Remembering his question, I yell through the wind, "It was amazing! I could hold my breath for so long, and I didn't get tired at all!"

The water continues to spray in my face, and my excited yelling mixes with laughter.

"There were so many fish and stingrays and sharks! They were swimming around me, and I could touch them! And I didn't feel afraid at all!"

Jesus laughs and shouts back over the roar of the boat cutting through the waves, "That's just the beginning! Wait until you're racing cheetahs across the African savanna, or swimming with orcas in Antarctica!"

Seeing my face light up with delight, Jesus laughs deeper and it echoes off the water.

Facing ahead, he continues maneuvering the sails.

We start going faster and faster.

I hold on tight.

Although the water looks enticing, I don't want to tumble overboard.

This is exhilarating, and to my surprise, I don't feel any fear.

I feel brave, like I can conquer anything.

The wind starts to die down again.

I notice Jesus making motions with his hand, and I realize he's been controlling the wind this whole time.

I walk over to him.

"It's so beautiful here. I don't ever want to leave."

Jesus looks at me with bright eyes and smiles.

He starts lowering the sails.

I glance around, searching for a way to help, when my eyes land on the journal resting on the seat beside me.

Jesus nods toward it with a smile. "Go ahead, Sammy. Your words are a treasure."

With everything still fresh in my mind, I sit down, heart full, wanting to capture it all before it fades.

I pick up the pen clipped to the side and begin to write.

As I write about my experience here off the coast of Whitsunday, I begin to wonder what it would be like to go to Whitsunday on Earth.

Would I enjoy it as much?

Or would it be tainted by all the brokenness in the world?

"It's every bit as beautiful," Jesus says, breaking through my thoughts.

I glance up. He's watching me with a sincere expression.

"You only need to keep your eyes open, Sammy. There's beauty all around you on Earth. Sin has damaged much, yes, but wonder still remains. You just have to be willing to see it."

I nod, though I'm not quite sure what he means.

My eyes are always open.

He smiles gently, clearly aware of my thoughts.

"You began to see it today," he says. "When you met a good friend of mine, Joshua. Your eyes were just beginning to open, but you shut them again out of fear."

I'm startled to hear Joshua mentioned, and I want to ask more about him, but Jesus continues speaking.

"The reason you see the beauty here is because there's no fear in Heaven. Without fear, you can finally see what's always been right in front of you. When you're a child, everything feels full of wonder. Your heart is open, your vision clear. But as you grow older, if you don't let me protect your heart, fear finds a way in. And fear clouds everything. Only perfect love can cast it out."

I start thinking about Joshua and how we sat together next to the tree.

I remember the small glimpse of hope that started to bubble in my chest, how everything suddenly felt a little brighter.

And I remember how quickly fear rushed in, gripping my chest like a claw.

Jesus was right. I closed my heart.

There was a small glimpse of hope, and I was afraid.

"It's just so much work," I admit softly. "Here, everything feels easy. There's no fear, because you're here with me. I'm not alone. But back home, there's so much pain. It's unbearable."

"Sammy, I have always been with you," Jesus says, his voice full of compassion. "Through all the pain, I've never left your side. I know it's hard to see, but my Father has a plan for you—a purpose."

He pauses, his eyes meeting mine, unwavering.

"I walked the earth as a man. I was tested in every way a person can be. I understand how hard it is. Even I asked my Father to take the suffering from me, but I chose to keep going. For his glory. Because in that moment, I saw the purpose of my life: to be the one who would save you, and all of mankind."

A tear slips down his cheek.

"Every ounce of pain was worth it. I'd do it all over again… just for you."

Jesus comes over and wraps me in a hug.

As I melt into his warmth, memories from childhood flood back, everything I ever learned about him.

How he walked the earth as a man.

How he healed the sick and set the captives free.

How he was hurt and persecuted.

How he never did anything wrong.

He was perfect.

And still they killed him… out of fear.

After meeting him and feeling his perfect love and kindness, the thought of what people did to him is too much.

Tears pour down my face.

How could anyone hurt him?

How could they do this to him?

The tears won't stop.

Jesus holds me tighter, gently rocking me as I sob into his chest, until the tears finally run dry.

All that's left is a deep, aching gratitude.

Gratitude for what he did.

For me.

If I return home or wake up from this dream, will I be able to see the beauty Jesus talked about? Will I be able to keep my eyes open and not let fear close them again?

I look up at the one who walked through pain and death for someone like me.

His eyes, shimmering with specks of gold and filled with love, make me believe anything is possible.

Jesus releases me and extends his hand, his face glowing with a breathtaking smile.

"Are you ready for our next adventure, Sammy?"

CHAPTER 9

*"Remember not the former things, nor consider the
things of old. Behold, I am doing a new thing; now
it springs forth, do you not perceive it? I will make
a way in the wilderness and rivers in the desert."*

ISAIAH 43:18-19 ESV

Grasping his hand, we step through a door.

I try to find a sign to see where we are going, but there isn't one.

Strange.

My right foot touches down on solid, rocky ground, my left soon to follow.

A fog is thick around me, and I feel a mist settle gently on my face. I can't see more than a foot in front of me. I squint, trying to see anything that would reveal where we are.

Light starts to break through the fog, the sun burning it away like it does every morning back home.

This looks strangely familiar.

It tickles at a memory: camping with my family when we were younger at a place far, far north in Maine.

Reality lands like a punch to the gut.

I look out from the rocky summit into the vast, deep blue of the Atlantic Ocean.

This is Cadillac Mountain in Acadia National Park.

And it's the last place I want to be.

I look around frantically for Jesus, wondering why he brought me here.

Where did he go? He was just holding my hand.

Wasn't he all-knowing?

Didn't he know that this wasn't where I wanted to go—ever? That it would bring up too much hurt?

Feeling overcome with sadness, I plop down on a pile of rocks, staring out over the water and trying to push away the images of my family.

Anger starts to rise, boiling up and forcing the sadness out like the sun burning through the fog.

Seething with self-hatred, I throw my hands in the air.

"Why God! I still don't understand!"

Against my will, my brain starts bringing up all the memories I'd buried deep down.

We came to Acadia when I was just seven years old—me, Stephen, and our parents.

We went hiking, swam in the freezing Atlantic, and camped beneath stars brighter than I'd ever seen anywhere else.

I'll never forget the lobster.

My mouth starts to water at the thought of the most scrumptious lobster I've ever had, *steaming fresh, smothered in butter.*

I remember my father made us all wear these giant plastic bibs.

I felt ridiculous until I looked around and saw the rest of my family wearing them too.

I chuckle at the image of my parents in those oversized bibs.

Of course, Stephen strutted around like it was the newest fashion trend.

He somehow made everything seem cool.

It had been the perfect trip.

It was so perfect that we planned a trip for when Stephen graduated high school.

That summer, we were supposed to come back here as a family to celebrate.

Everything had already been mapped out, but Stephen died just two weeks before the trip.

My mother canceled it, and that was just the beginning of my life falling apart.

It was my fault the trip got canceled.

My eyes start to sting with fresh tears as I think about what life would be like if Stephen had never died.

We would have taken that trip.

Life would still be good.

Mother would still love me.

Father would be home.

I could never forgive myself for what happened.

I no longer feel like sitting here, staring out at the panoramic view of scattered islands and the deep indigo waters of the Gulf of Maine.

The sunlight reflects off the surface, making it sparkle.

It hurts my heart to see such beauty when my life is in absolute shambles.

Dusting myself off, I realize I need to get out of here.

Walking toward a marked path down the mountain, I search for a door.

Surely there must be a door I can walk through to get back to Heaven.

I kick a loose rock ahead in frustration, sending it skittering across the ground.

That's when I feel it, a warm sensation spreading from my head to my toes.

I don't even have to look. I know.

It's Jesus.

Just a few feet away, I see him.

His eyes meet mine, and the intensity of love is too much.

I look down, my face burning with shame.

How can I look into the eyes of someone perfect when I am the reason my brother died?

Jesus closes the distance between us and holds out his hand.

"Sammy, let's take a walk together."

Side by side, we begin walking along the winding path down the mountain, the deep green forest stretching around us is a striking contrast to the bright blue ocean beyond.

I keep my gaze fixed on the trail so I won't trip, which conveniently keeps me from having to meet his eyes.

After a while, Jesus speaks first.

"Why do you think I brought you here?"

I'm not sure what to say.

It feels like he brought me here as some kind of punishment, but I probably shouldn't say that out loud.

I knew it was too good to be true when he said I could have the gift of grace.

Of course, there's a catch.

A personal hell, where I have to relive all the bad things I've done.

Jesus nods slowly in understanding.

I forgot. He can perceive my thoughts.

Even still, he waits for me to answer him.

Feeling like I should just get it over with, I finally speak.

"I don't know… maybe you brought me here to punish me for killing my brother."

Saying it out loud feels like a punch to the chest.

"When you said we were going on another adventure, I didn't think you meant a place that would drag me back through everything I've tried to forget."

I glance at him, too ashamed to fully meet his gaze.

But his eyes, they're not the same.

They burn with holy fire so intense, I can't look away.

My head pounds as a rush of fierce love and holy anger floods my mind.

I clutch my head. "Make it stop," I whisper. *It's too much to feel.*

"Who made you believe you're the reason for Stephen's death?" he asks. "Who told you that lie, Sammy?"

His voice booms, echoing off the massive granite boulders we've been stepping over, weaving through patches of pine and stone on our way down the mountain.

He stops me in my tracks and grabs my hand.

Instantly, the overwhelming sensations leave my mind.

The fire fades from his eyes, and he gently squeezes my hand.

"Listen to what I say. You didn't kill your brother. And even though your parents treat you the way they do, you are not to blame."

He looks away, and another flash of anger crosses his face before it's replaced by the kindness I'm coming to know.

"Sammy, the same one who's been trying to destroy all the good I have planned for you is the one yelling lies at you every single day. That's not the voice of truth you're hearing. The world is broken. Until I return, there will be death. There will be imperfect people who choose to let anger consume them instead of surrendering their pain and receiving the peace I so freely offer."

My heart starts to feel like it's being ripped out of my chest.

Pain and peace battle inside me, and I cry out.

"Let the pain go, Sammy. The longer you hold onto it, the more it will hurt you."

I can't just let it go. My brother is dead because of me. I drop to the forest floor, torn between disbelief and desperation.

Jesus is beside me, holding me in his arms. "Let it go, Sammy. You were never meant to carry this. Give it to me. I will gladly take it."

Through the pain, I grit my teeth and whisper to myself, *it isn't my fault.*

Over and over again, I repeat those four words, hoping that the more I say them, the more I'll believe them.

I hold out my hands like I saw Jesus do.

And even though I don't fully believe it yet, I want to trust Jesus more than I trust myself.

After everything he's shown me, how could I not?

Slowly, I feel my heart begin to beat normally again.

Warmth fills my chest, and the pain that was crippling me vanishes.

I look up into Jesus' eyes, dark like the night sky, full of stars. They shine with love and compassion.

I don't know if this feeling will last or if the pain will creep back in, but for the first time, I feel a little lighter. A little more okay.

Jesus gives me a big hug and whispers that he's proud of me. I wipe the tears from my face with the back of my hand, take a deep breath, and let it out slowly.

He lifts me to my feet, and something catches my eye shimmering in the sunlight from a giant boulder.

It looks like... a mirror?

Why is that there?

"Sammy, come with me. You need to see something," Jesus says.

I slip my fingers into his and follow him over the rocks toward it.

Sure enough, a tall mirror is built into the side of the boulder, reflecting the forest around us.

I hang back, standing just far enough to the side so I don't have to see myself.

"Sammy, I want you to look at yourself," Jesus says gently. "I want you to see what I see."

I glance at him, eyes wide, embarrassment rushing to my cheeks. I already know what he sees: a tall, too-thin girl with hair falling out and eyes that feel hollow.

I don't need to witness that. Not here, not with him.

Here, I want to pretend I'm someone else.

"Trust me," he says softly, releasing my hand.

I smooth down my hair, trying to fix what little I can. I take a small step to the left until I'm directly in front of the mirror. My eyes squeeze shut.

I take a breath.

Then I peek one open just a sliver.

Oh my…

Both eyes fly open.

Staring back at me… is me.

Still tall, still thin, still awkwardly lanky, but somehow… I look beautiful.

Nothing about me has changed. My hair is still thinning. But the soft brown actually suits me. It makes my green eyes pop. I've never noticed how bright they are.

Have they always been that green?

They used to look so dull.

The freckles across my nose make me look… interesting. Like they belong.

And there's a soft glow coming from around me. Like what I saw with Marie.

I feel Jesus beside me. I glance up at him, confused and overwhelmed. He smiles.

"Your heart is gold, Sammy. It pours out of you, and it shines. You only ever look at the surface, but I see what's inside. And now, you can too."

I turn back to the mirror, staring into my own bright, green eyes. *Wow. Maybe I'm not as bad as I think.*

Jesus puts his arm around my shoulder, giving it a tight squeeze.

A sinking feeling settles in my stomach. Our adventure in Heaven is coming to an end.

I cling to him, not ready to let go.

"Samantha Jane," he says gently. "It's time. Don't forget what you've seen. The glory that awaits. But your story isn't finished yet. There's still more for you back home."

He looks deeply into my eyes and gives me one final, heart-healing hug.

"I'll be interceding for you, talking to my Father on your behalf. His plans for you are good. Trust me."

I don't want to let go. I start to protest, but before I can say a word, there's a flash of light.

And just like that, I'm no longer in the middle of Acadia with Jesus.

I'm not in Cappadocia meeting him for the first time, nor am I swimming with sharks off the coast of the Whitsundays.

I'm back in the tunnel of light with Marie, leaving the place I never thought actually existed. Returning to the place I wish didn't exist.

CHAPTER 10

"The light shines in the darkness,
and the darkness has not overcome it."

JOHN 1:5 ESV

"Goodbye, Sammy. I'll be cheering you on," I hear Marie's distant voice as I shoot up in bed.

The room is completely dark. My clock glows, and my stomach drops when I see the time: *12:01 AM.*

What? No, that can't be. I was in Heaven. With Jesus. I left at midnight. So how has only a minute passed?

My eyes adjust to the darkness, and I look around for a sign, or maybe some angel dust, if that's even a thing. Anything to prove that I had left. *Had it all been a vivid, wonderful dream? But I met Jesus. It felt so real... our conversations, the adventures.*

Was my mind just pulling up something from deep in my memories? I have been more reflective these past few days. Maybe because of that, my brain conjured up the most wild, beautiful dream of my life.

I kick off my covers and quickly walk over to my mirror.

I'm met with dull, lifeless eyes. My brown hair is matted to my face. There's no glow. My freckles look splotchy and not charming.

It was just a dream.

With heaviness, I make my way back to bed.

Lying there, staring at the ceiling, I'm overcome with a sense of loss like I just experienced what life was meant to be, and now it's gone.

A thick heaviness settles over me and over the whole room.

I suddenly feel like I can't breathe.

Chills run up my body, goosebumps freckling my arms and legs.

My gaze is drawn to the corner, where an old rocking chair sits.

My heart starts racing as I see the outline of a man.

No, not a man.

A creature, sitting in the chair.

I throw the blanket over my head, fear coursing through my veins as I silently beg whatever it is to leave. But the image is burned into my mind: the dark silhouette, the horns protruding from its head.

Click, clack. Click, clack.

It's moving.

Not away from me, but toward me.

Click, clack. Click, clack.

Claws tap against the floor, slow and deliberate, inching closer with every sound.

The closer it gets, I start to hear a voice in my head, sharp and venomous.

"IT WASN'T REAL."

I am frozen in place, paralyzed by terror.

I want to scream for help. *Would my mother come?*

I don't know what to do or what I'm up against.

My throat tightens, the air thinning like it's being sucked from the room.

I feel hot breath press through the thin layer of my blanket.

I'm out of time.

So I do the only thing I can.

I cry out to the friend I met in my dream, desperately willing him to be real.

"Jesus," I whisper. It's barely more than a breath, but air rushes back into my lungs.

I peek out from under the blanket, expecting to see the horned creature inches from my face, but there's nothing there.

I exhale, body still trembling.

What was that thing?

All I know is it wasn't good.

Maybe the food deprivation is finally catching up to me.

Lucid dreams. Hallucinations.

Great.

Throwing the blankets back over my head, I sink into my pillow, overcome with exhaustion. *Maybe this is all a dream, and if I just lay here and close my eyes, I'll fall back into the good one—the one about Heaven.*

I drift off, expecting to be shuffled through a tunnel of light, back to the place called Heaven.

My alarm beeps. *It's 5 A.M.*

Life feels strangely normal, as if I didn't just go to Heaven, hang out with Jesus on grand adventures, and then come back to my room where I was terrorized by a creature from another world.

I realize how crazy that sounds.

I hit my pillow hard, over and over, until it's flat as a pancake.

Frustration pours out of me.

It wasn't real. None of it was.

Why does my heart fight me on it, though? It felt real last night. I was convinced I had met Jesus. Then there was Marie, and the hot air balloons in Turkey, swimming with all the sea creatures off the coast of the Whitsundays, sailing through the multicolored waters, and that wild experience in the middle of the forest in Acadia.

A dry laugh escapes my lips. *Of course that wasn't real! As if that's what Heaven is like and Jesus just wanted to hang out with Sammy-nobody from Maine.*

I feel completely embarrassed. I'm now a crazy person that believes she went to Heaven when it was only a dream. Joshua must have gotten in my head with all his "God talk," and that's why this happened.

It was a nice dream. And for a moment, I thought life would get better. That I could believe what Jesus told me. But the truth is, it wasn't real. I am now back in my living nightmare. Nothing has changed.

The heavy weight of dread fills me as I flop back into bed—the same feeling I had when I dreamed of that creature watching me from the corner of my room. I shiver. *That was one bad dream.*

I grab my journal off the nightstand, and a sharp pang of disappointment hits me. It's not the one from Heaven. The beautiful, leather-bound one with the inscription. That journal would've proved it wasn't just a dream. But of course, it's not here. Just more evidence it wasn't real.

I flip to an empty page and sigh.

Dear Universe,

What are you doing to me? Can't you just leave me alone?
I was ready. But then that dream… it felt so real. I want to
believe what I saw. What I felt. I want to believe that Jesus
held me in his arms. That he was real. So real. The people
I saw there… they weren't alone. I want to believe I'm not
either. But every time I start to feel a flicker of hope, it gets
crushed. I'm tired. I can't keep up. I just want to feel happy.
I just want to feel happy…

Sincerely confused,
Sammy

P.S. What did I see in my room?!

CHAPTER 11

*"Elijah was a man with a nature like ours, and he prayed
fervently that it might not rain, and for three years and
six months it did not rain on the earth. Then he prayed
again, and heaven gave rain, and the earth bore its fruit."*

JAMES 5:17-18 ESV

Joshua isn't on the bus today, which is odd since it's only his second day at school. I was hoping to tell him about the crazy dream I had. I think he'd be the only one who might actually understand why it shook me so deeply.

I really need to talk to someone.

The bus slowly creaks down the road, the wheels feel as if they are moving in slow motion. The bumps jar me against the window, and I wince in pain.

Finally, we pull into the parking lot, and I make my way off the bus. Everything looks dull. The laughter from my classmates feels shallow. The contrast from my dream to reality is frustrating.

I pull my hoodie I grabbed on the way out the door tighter around my face, trying to keep my face hidden.

Mother was on an exceptional rampage this morning. I have the mark to commemorate her rage. The makeup covers it well enough, but I don't want anyone asking questions about the bruise. If anyone found out, things at home would only get worse.

She doesn't normally hit, but I had reached for an apple without asking if I was allowed to have one. *Heaven forbid I eat an apple without her permission.* Her hand flew across my face before I could even blink.

"You really think you deserve anything? Your chores aren't done, your grades are slipping! Nothing changes! In my house, you ask before you take. Got it?"

All I could do was hang my head low, tears stinging my eyes, and squeak out, "Yes, ma'am."

What stung more than the slap was her taking the apple and throwing it in the trash.

Sent off to school, another morning without anything to eat.

Sometimes, I wish my father would come home just so they could yell at each other for a while and take the focus off of me. It's no wonder he lives for his work so much so that he basically lives at his office. Our house is full of misery now. No one wants to be there.

And I'm the only one who's going to do something about it. Because I don't see the point of living in misery.

The morning is a wake-up call. I'm convinced now that last night was just a dream. There's no way I actually went to Heaven. If it were real, why didn't Jesus let me stay? Why would he send me back to my own personal hell? No… it couldn't have been real.

And yet, something is gnawing at my heart, stirring deep in my soul, and it's taking everything in me to silence it. The "what if" is strong in my mind.

Let it go, Sam. It wasn't real.

Pushing the thoughts away, I'm almost to the door when I see Joshua standing off to the side of the building. His head is resting against the wall, eyes closed, a smile on his face. *He looks so peaceful, genuinely happy.*

I hesitate, my heart pounding in my chest.

For a moment, I debate whether I should go over.

I don't know what's compelling me, but I start walking.

Maybe it's because I'm bursting to tell someone what I experienced last night, desperate for reassurance that it was just a dream.

Or maybe, I'm hoping he'll tell me it was real.

Before I reach him, his eyes open and he looks my way, a big eye-crinkling grin spreading across his face.

"Sammy!"

I smile, just slightly, wondering how someone can be so excited all the time. The only place I've ever seen this kind of joy… was in my dream. In Heaven. Where joy felt abundant.

Even laughing with Jesus made life feel exciting, even if all we were doing was sitting under a tree. Life felt simple, but complete. Because I had Jesus by my side.

Why couldn't that have been real?

"I was hoping to see you this morning."

Joshua throws his arm around my shoulders, grabs the books weighing me down, and starts walking with me toward the door.

I blush, caught off guard by the fact that he was hoping to see me.

We walk in silence, comfortable for him maybe, but I'm keenly aware of a certain boy's arm draped over my shoulders. *It isn't entirely unwelcome, I just hope no one is watching us.* The thought alone makes my face turn several shades pinker.

I steal a glance at Joshua, wondering if he's as affected as I am. He's watching me with that same kind smile, and my blush deepens. His grin grows wider, a flicker of victory flashing across his face before he casually drops his arm from my shoulder.

Relief washes over me, but so does a strange sense of loss.

"You weren't on the bus," I blurt.

I'm not sure why I said that. It's an obvious fact, but I feel the need to break the silence.

"Yeah," he says with a laugh. "I was up early and decided some fresh air would be nice, so I walked."

"I didn't know if I'd like it here compared to California," he says, glancing around. "But these early spring days are beautiful. The sun shining on us, the birds chirping, being surrounded by so much nature, it really beats the city smog."

He pauses for a second, "I really think I'm going to like it here."

He grins at me before continuing. "And then there's this cool girl I met. I definitely think I'm going to like it here." He chuckles, cheeks flushing slightly.

I can't help but smile. He's honest and just says how he feels. It's refreshing and honestly, kind of shocking. I'm not used to people like him.

I know I need to tell him about my dream. He's the only person I've met who talks about God so openly. Maybe, he'll understand. Nervously, I glance at Joshua and ask, "Do you want to eat lunch together today?"

His face lights up into a huge grin. "Yeah! Let's do it."

. . .

The morning is dragging by. First period is usually my favorite. I love spending time writing and learning, but today, I just want to skip ahead to lunch. And as if the universe knows how anxious I am, second and third period crawl by even slower. *If I don't talk to Joshua about this soon, I'm going to scream!*

Finally, the bell rings for lunch, and I'm out the door, basically running to the cafeteria. I grab my lunch and pay as quickly as I can before heading to the giant pine. I know Joshua will be there.

Briskly crossing the yard, Joshua appears beside me out of nowhere. I jump, nearly dropping my tray.

I let out a small shriek.

"Seriously, Joshua? Don't you know not to sneak up on someone like that?"

Joshua laughs. "Hey, I called your name. Multiple times actually. You were so focused on that pine tree, I figured you must've seen an angel or something."

He gives me a wink and a smirk, then takes off running.

I stop short.

An angel? That's an odd thing to say. But then again, it's Joshua and he's already proving to be a unique character. Still, being near him makes me feel like something in me is shifting.

I break into a run to catch up with him. He really loves to run, apparently. I'm breathless by the time I plop down in the lush grass beside him. The spring rains are already bringing everything to life earlier than normal for Maine. A patch of wildflowers is starting to bud nearby.

They remind me of the ones I saw in Heaven.

In my dream, that is.

I'm trying to figure out how to bring it up to Joshua. Do I just blurt it out and hope he doesn't think I'm crazy?

He reaches for his food, and his sleeve slips back slightly revealing scar tissue in the shape of a circle.

That doesn't look good.

Joshua notices me staring and gives a small shrug, quietly pulling his sleeve back down.

"Some things just don't make sense on earth."

I look up and meet his eyes. For the first time, there's a trace of sadness in them, but also something else I can't quite place.

Joshua glances at my cheekbone, then reaches out and gently touches it.

I wince.

His face immediately scrunches in understanding.

"I'm sorry."

Those two words are filled with kindness, they touch something deep inside me, threatening to break through the walls I've worked so hard to build.

"I'm sorry you have to feel that pain. I know what it's like to try and hide the marks. Unfortunately, guys wearing makeup isn't exactly accepted."

He lets out a quiet chuckle, but it isn't his usual one. This laugh is laced with pain.

All I can do is nod, a lump forming in my throat. I turn away and stare at my lunch, not sure what to say. Joshua is the last person I expected this from. He seems so happy, but maybe he's living a life just as painful as mine, or maybe even worse. *How can someone be filled with that much joy while carrying so much pain?*

"Hey Sammy, I don't want to make you uncomfortable, but would it be okay if I prayed before we eat? It's something I usually like to do."

I feel a little awkward, but one prayer won't hurt. He even asked. I don't know anyone who's ever shown me this much kindness.

I fold my hands and bow my head, not sure what the proper etiquette is. I peek one eye open to see what Joshua is doing.

His eyes are open, palms facing upward, and he starts more informally than I expected.

"Hi God. Joshua and Sammy here—well, you already know that. Thank you for this beautiful day, for another breath in our lungs. Thank you for my new friend, Sammy, and for reminding us that we're never alone. Please protect her. Fill her heart with your love, the kind she used to know. Fill us both with your joy and peace, and help us never forget the glory that's waiting on the other side. In Jesus' name, amen."

"Amen," I repeat, a lump rising in my throat.

No one has ever prayed for me before.

Joshua laughs and lets out a big, "Wahoo!" jolting me out of my thoughts.

"He's so good, Sammy. So good. I just love him." He sighs, grinning. "Now let's eat, I'm starved."

Joshua dives into his food. I slowly join in, hunger rising, but his prayer keeps echoing in my mind. *Not only did he pray for me, he called me his friend.*

This isn't good. I won't be here much longer. I can't afford to let anyone see me that way. Not now. That could ruin everything.

What else did he say in that prayer? Something about filling me with the love I once knew? Was he referencing last night? Did he know? Did he somehow slip me a drug yesterday that caused me to hallucinate? Is that why he keeps winking and dropping hints?

I turn to speak to him, but just as I open my mouth, he bursts into laughter and he doesn't stop. He just keeps laughing and laughing. I sit there, dumbfounded. As usual.

Finally, he wipes away tears and looks at me, grinning. "I'm sorry, I should've said something first thing this morning. I know this might sound weird, but... I know where you were last night. I was hoping you'd tell me yourself, but I couldn't keep it in any longer."

He flops onto his back and stares up at the sky, as if he's somewhere else entirely, his face lit by a memory. "Wasn't it glorious, Sammy?"

I freeze, stunned that he knows, but anger quickly rises to meet the shock. He's right, this is weird.

How does he know what happened? Did he sneak into my house? Watch me sleep? Was I mumbling in my sleep?

The thought fills me with rage.

"How do you know this? Did you come to my house?" My voice shakes. "Tell me right now or I'm calling the cops."

Before I can continue yelling, Joshua sits up quickly and looks me right in the eyes.

I'm caught off guard for a moment, completely lost in his warm brown eyes flecked with gold. I never noticed the gold before.

"Oh no, absolutely not! I would never do that," Joshua says, his eyes wide. "Let me explain."

He looks nervous but speaks with quiet certainty. "The reason I know what happened is because I prayed for it. Yesterday, when I met you, I could see it—the pain in your eyes, the weight you were carrying, how little hope you had. I've been there, Sammy. I knew I had to ask God to help you."

His voice grows stronger. "So, I prayed that he would show you a glimpse of glory, like he did for me."

His eyes glisten, but he doesn't hide the tears. "I know how faithful he is to our prayers. I just… knew he would show up."

Then, his face breaks into a soft, triumphant smile. "He did, didn't he?"

I stare in disbelief, slowly shaking my head as I try to make sense of it all.

Could he actually be telling the truth?

I look up at Joshua and there is a pureness to him that makes me believe him. The anger melts away as I realize it just might have been real.

"Yeah… he did. I thought it was just a dream…"

He laughs, his voice shifting into excitement. "So, what did you see? Did you go to the Amazon? You should've seen me and Jesus marching through the rainforest, machetes in hand, cutting through vines, wading past snakes and gators. We laughed so much. It was wild."

My jaw drops open. I didn't think it was possible to be shocked anymore, but Joshua just did it.

"Hold up, I'm still lost. You're telling me that after meeting me you prayed I'd see Heaven? And not only that, but you've been there too?"

He grins that big, eye-crinkling grin. "Yep! I don't know how else to explain it. It didn't make sense to me either when it happened. I stopped asking how and why. I just know it was real. I want to hear about your adventure. Will you share it with me?"

Still stunned, I tell Joshua everything: my trip to Heaven, my mother, my father, Stephen. It all spills out, and it feels good to finally share.

I leave out the part about ending it all and the weird creature in my room. He doesn't need to know that.

For today, I'll share my story and my adventure in Heaven with Joshua.

Soon enough, I'll be gone. And he'll forget I was ever here.

But for the first time in a long time, I don't feel completely alone.

CHAPTER 12

*"I am hard pressed between the two. My desire is to
depart and be with Christ, for that is far better. But to
remain in the flesh is more necessary on your account."*

PHILIPPIANS 1:23 ESV

The first bell rings, signaling lunch is coming to an end. I stop mid-sentence, my cheeks flushing.

I just spilled my entire story to a stranger.

Joshua's been listening quietly the whole time, gently encouraging me to keep going, even through the really hard parts.

I grab my tray and start picking up the trash, the silence between us suddenly thick. The regret hits me almost instantly.

"Thank you for sharing with me, Sammy. I know that wasn't easy."

He gives me a soft smile, and I return it, just barely.

He holds out his hand. I take it, and he hoists me to my feet.

My steps feel lighter as I walk toward the door.

A quiet relief washes over me.

Someone knows my story.

Just before we walk through the doors, Joshua turns to me, his face missing the smile I've grown used to.

He rubs the back of his neck nervously before speaking softly.

"Are you going to stay, Sammy?"

I freeze, trying not to show how much his question rattles me.

"You met Jesus," he continues. "Do you trust him?"

My stomach twists into instant knots. I can't admit it. So, I play dumb and hope he'll drop it.

"I don't know what you're talking about."

Joshua sighs. "Come on, Sammy. Please don't lie to me. I saw it in your eyes, clear as day. And I just had this knowing. This urgency in my heart yesterday to pray for you. I knew why, because I've been there too."

He looks away, and for the first time, I see him trying to hide something from me.

When he meets my eyes again, they're full of compassion, and I know I can't lie to him.

"Joshua, it doesn't change anything."

I nervously pick at my fingernails, trying to keep my emotions in check.

"I don't even know if what I experienced was real. I know you said you had something similar, but… what if it was just a dream? For both of us?"

I pause, my voice dropping. "And if it wasn't a dream, then I want to be there. Sooner."

Frustrated, I sigh.

"This life has nothing to offer but pain. Why wouldn't I want to go there instead of staying here?"

I turn and walk inside, leaving Joshua behind as the door closes between us.

The single teardrop trailing down his face etches itself into my memory.

That should be enough to make him leave me alone now.

. . .

The evening passes by with its usual dramatic flair. Mother freaks out about something, and I go to bed hungry. I change into my pajamas and crawl into my warm bed, thankful I still have it. I'm especially drained tonight, worn out by the emotional chaos of the day.

The image of Joshua threatens to surface every time I close my eyes, his eyes filled with so much sadness. *Why does he care? It's ruining everything.* I force the image away and, after tossing and turning for hours, finally drift off to sleep. No expectations of dreams. Certainly not ones about Heaven.

But piercing through my sleep is a bright light.

My first thought is that Mother's turned on my bedroom light and that I'm in trouble for something. I open my eyes quickly, fear slicing through me, ready for the yelling or worse.

But standing at the foot of my bed isn't my mother.

It's Marie.

Her whimsical voice, which I was sure I'd made up in a dream, breaks through the stillness of the night.

"Sammy, wake up. It's time to go back to Heaven."

She glows radiantly. I'm just as stunned as the first time.

Seeing that I'm not moving, she smiles gently and continues.

"There have been urgent prayers lifted for you. Normally, we don't do repeat visits," she adds with a sparkle in her eye, "but you have a friend who really, really cares."

She smiles. "Joshua has always been special, always looking out for his friends. But this time is different. He won't stop praying. The throne room is overflowing with his prayers. Jesus has been interceding nonstop on your behalf, and the Father has made an exception. He's inviting you back for one more visit."

Her voice softens as she leans forward. "So, hurry up. Let's go."

Before I even have time to react, we're back in the tunnel of light, everything swirling around us, time ending and eternity beginning.

Marie's voice echoes in my mind as I'm pulled forward.

"We have something very special for you tonight."

I embrace the void of time in the tunnel. Weightless, I reach out and let my fingers graze the colorful walls around me. At the slightest touch, joy electrifies my body. Laughter spills out of me. Pure, uncontrollable. And I'm left feeling elated.

Then, suddenly, we arrive.

The golden city stretches before me once again, more breathtaking than I remembered. This time, it's not the sight that greets me first, it's the sound. Music. Glorious music. There must be hundreds of instruments forming a grand orchestra, their melodies weaving together into a symphony, as if announcing my arrival.

I'm lost in it, caught up in the beauty and wonder. For a moment, I forget my confusion. I forget I ever questioned whether this place was real. I have a thousand questions swirling in my mind, but Marie speaks first.

"Sammy, don't worry. In time, you'll understand. For now, someone is waiting to see you."

She smiles and starts walking. "Follow me."

We walk through the city, waving at familiar faces from the other day. I see the little girl that called me pretty playing with her friends. They chase each other around, laughing, not needing anything but friendship. *I desperately want to be that happy.*

We reach the center of the city, where the vast garden stretches out before us. The flowers are different today, lilies sprouting everywhere. The smell is intoxicating and I feel my whole body relax. Closing my eyes, I breathe in deeply.

When I open them, I come face-to-face with a small, shimmering hummingbird painted blue and green like a tropical ocean. I hold out my hand in wonder and it pauses just long enough to rest on my finger before darting off to pollinate another flower.

A laugh slips from my lips, and I catch the eye of a woman planting flowers nearby. She gives me a wide smile and a wave before returning to her work.

The doors begin to appear, but they're different this time. More vague. Instead of specific places, they simply say: *The Mountains. The Ocean. The Forest. The Desert.*

I definitely won't be picking The Desert. I've never liked the heat.

But one door catches my eye.

The Meadow.

I've always been obsessed with meadows, ever since I was little. Stephen and I used to run through them, arms stretched wide, letting our fingers skim the tall grass.

The memory hits hard and sadness wells up in my chest.

I shake it off. I'm not ready to think about Stephen right now.

I want to feel happiness, and I have a feeling *The Meadow* will do just that.

I say my goodbyes to Marie, this time feeling a lot more confident knowing that only good things wait on the other side. At least, I hope.

The door swings open and before me is a meadow that stretches for miles without an end in sight. The grass is up to my waist, swaying in the gentle breeze. Birds fly overhead and I'm mesmerized as they form patterns, dancing in sync across the sky. The grass is dotted with so many wildflowers that the meadow looks pink, purple, white, and yellow with only specks of green here and there. It's breathtaking to watch all the colors glimmer in the sun.

I start picking them to create a wild bouquet. I'm not sure if I can take it back to Earth, but they're too perfect not to pick.

I prance along without a care in the world, running my fingers through the blades of grass when I hear his bold, boisterous laugh that calls to my heart. *Jesus.*

I turn to see him standing a few feet behind me.

"Sammy!" he cries. "You're here! How delightful it is to see you!"

I run to him. He picks me up in his arms and spins me around, both of us laughing and crying with delight. It's something my father used to do when I was a little girl.

"You're real," I whisper, touching his face. My fingers meet warm skin. *He isn't a hallucination. This isn't a dream. This is Jesus and he is real.*

Jesus chuckles, "Of course I'm real, Sammy. And everything you experienced last night was real too." His expression softens. "I heard from a friend that you've been having some doubts. Do you want to talk about them?"

I feel ashamed to have doubted once again, but there's no judgment in Jesus' eyes, only compassion.

"I wasn't sure it was real," I admit, my voice trembling. "I didn't think it could be, because it's perfect here, but you made me go back to Earth, where my life is not. Why did you make me leave?"

Tears form in my eyes. I try my best to hold them in, but they won't listen. They spill over, one by one. Jesus reaches up and catches the first tear as it falls. It evaporates from his hand, lifting into a soft mist, just like last time.

He leans in close and speaks gently. "For I know the plans I have for you, plans to prosper you and not to harm you, plans to give you hope and a future."

Jesus holds my gaze.

"I couldn't let you stay here, Sammy. If I had, you would've missed out on the good plans still waiting for you."

I clench and unclench my hands.

"What plans? The ones where I starve every day? Where my mother keeps getting worse? Or maybe the ones where I get bullied nonstop? How could anything good come out of that?"

I don't even realize I'm yelling, but Jesus isn't fazed. He meets me with steady empathy, his voice calm and full of understanding.

"I have felt the same," he says. "That night in the garden, when I was praying, I was gripped by fear. I begged my Father to take it from me. I was mocked, beaten, and nailed to a cross. The pain was so intense, I could barely remember the promises the Father made to me."

His eyes fill with tears.

"But with all my strength, I pulled those promises to the front of my heart. And for the glory that you and all who would believe in me would one day experience, I surrendered."

He gently wipes away the tears trailing down my cheek.

"My dear Sammy. I know what it feels like to believe it will never get better, to think you won't survive it. But it will. And you will."

New tears pour out and I collapse in the arms of Jesus, silently praying. *Help me to believe!*

Jesus holds me tighter.

"I will help you," he whispers. "I know you've felt alone for a long time, maybe even doubting if I'm truly your friend."

He smiles softly.

"But there was a time when you called me your friend."

I look up at him, confused. *I know I used to believe he was real, but I don't recall ever calling him that.*

"Sammy, when you were just five years old, you'd lay outside on your favorite pink checkered blanket. A pile of books always sat beside you, teetering and ready to fall. You'd lie there for hours, pretending to read out loud, acting out each character you saw."

My heart starts to race. The memories flood back. *Oh, how I had loved that pink blanket, so warm and fuzzy, like a hug.*

"You'd read your books and then talk to the air," Jesus continues, "as if you were talking to a best friend. Your parents would ask who you were reading to, and you'd always say, 'My friend.'"

Full clarity hits me. I remember it like it was yesterday. I had always felt like someone was there with me. When a book made me cry, a gentle breeze would dry my tears. When one made me laugh so hard I rolled in the grass, a warmth filled my heart. I never felt alone.

"I was there with you, Sammy," Jesus says gently. "The gentle breeze. The warmth. It was me. I've always been with you, even when you stopped believing."

I hug him tightly.

"Remember that, Sammy. When you feel alone, remember me."

He gives me a final squeeze, then lets me go.

"And now, my friend, I want you to see someone."

My interest is piqued. *Who could he possibly want me to see?*

Jesus gives me a huge, mischievous grin, then takes off running across the field.

That's when I see him. Another man running beside Jesus, arms skimming the grass like we used to.

My breath catches. I break into a run.

My heart pounds in my chest and I will my legs to move faster.

I don't dare take my eyes off him, terrified he might vanish.

"Stephen!" I cry out. *Please… let it be him.*

He stops suddenly. So does Jesus.

Jesus turns first, eyes beaming, smile wide, and gives me a wink. In that moment, I know.

The man turns next and smiles.

"Hey, Sammy."

CHAPTER 13

I slide to a stop a few feet from him, frozen in disbelief.

Stephen.

Time stands still. The breeze quiets. The meadow doesn't move. And neither do I.

Then, like a horse out of the gate, I bolt into his arms.

The strength of his embrace wraps around my back, filling my heart with the sense of belonging I haven't felt since he left.

I grab his face in my hands, just like I did with Jesus. I need to be sure he's real and that I'm not hallucinating. My brain still fights me, whispering that this can't be.

"It's you, Stephen. It's really you."

Tears pour down my face as I begin to sob.

"Hey now, kid. Don't cry," he says gently. "I'm here. Look at me. I'm alright. Better than alright."

I search his blue eyes for the truth, needing to see it for myself. And I do. Joy radiates from him. Undeniable, unshakable joy. *He isn't just okay. He's perfect.*

As if to prove it, he spins around a couple of times.

"Look at me, I'm stunning!"

I let out a laugh between sobs. *Classic Stephen. Always finding a way to make me laugh.*

Standing before me is my brother. Glowing with life. His body is healed, not a single scratch.

The sobs keep coming, the weight of his death hitting me again and again.

"I just don't… don't understand," I stammer, choking on my own emotion as I try to steady my breathing.

"What don't you understand, Sammy?" he asks, like this is the most normal thing in the world.

Pulling myself together a little more, I take Stephen's hand in mine and grip it tight, never wanting to let go.

"How are you here, Stephen?" I whisper. "Did you know this actually existed?"

Shaking my head, I add, "I didn't. Not really. Not until recently. And even now, I don't understand how I'm here."

Stephen squeezes my hand tighter, grounding me in the moment.

"I guess I've got some explaining to do," he says with a small smile, rubbing the back of his neck. "There's more to my story than you knew."

He chuckles softly, but there's a crack in his voice.

"I always kind of believed in God. We went to church when you were little, remember?"

I do remember. Seeing Jesus brought it all back.

"Well, I had faith back then, but I lost it over the years. Our family stopped going to church, and God just… wasn't mentioned again. My friends were great, but they didn't believe, so I stopped pursuing it too."

He grips my hand.

"But in eighth grade, someone invited me to a Bible study at school. I didn't tell anyone. I was embarrassed. I wasn't even sure what I believed anymore."

A smile lights up his face, his eyes suddenly bright.

"But that's where I met him. The real Jesus. The one you met here."

His eyes mist over and he swallows hard as the memories come flooding back.

"That's when I heard the gospel for the first time… and I believed it. That's why I'm here, Sammy. Because I believed in Jesus. I gave my life to him and he saved me."

He pauses, pain flickering across his face.

"I wanted to tell the family, especially you. But I chickened out. My biggest regret is not telling you the truth before I died."

He wipes his eyes and looks deep into mine.

"I prayed for you. And for Mom and Dad. I prayed so much."

I don't know what to say. I'm blindsided.

Stephen had believed all this time.

I wish he had told me. I wish I had known.

I look up at him, my chest aching.

I've missed him so much.

For a moment, we stand there, brother and sister, reunited.

One broken.

One made whole.

I want to be made whole too.

The air begins to shift. Warmth and a soft tingling spread through my body.

As if on cue, Jesus appears, walking toward us.

He places a hand on Stephen's shoulder, the way someone might greet an old friend.

With tears in his eyes and a smile on his face, Jesus says, "It brings me joy to see you two reunited."

He places his other hand on my shoulder and gives it a gentle squeeze.

"I'm going to take a walk in the sunshine, but if you need me, you know where to find me."

He looks directly at me. There's a mixture of pain and hope in his eyes.

Is he carrying my pain again? As if to answer my silent question, a peace washes over me so deep and steady it settles into my bones.

Jesus walks away, slowly drifting through the meadow, singing a song. The birds join in, creating a gentle melody. The air feels lighter. The colors around me brighten. I close my eyes, a smile filling my face.

I turn to Stephen suddenly aware that our time together might be short.

"I miss you so much. Everything has changed since you left."

Unable to meet his eyes, I stare down at the ground.

"I'm sorry you died saving me. I'm so sorry."

The tears spill faster than I can stop them. Stephen pulls me into a big bear hug, stroking my hair just like he used to when I fell off my bike and skinned my knee.

"Hey, don't cry. God redeems all things. I'd choose to save you all over again."

His voice is calm. His steady heartbeat echoes beneath my ear. I take a deep breath and let myself relax.

"All things work together for the good of those who love God."

He looks into my eyes and his expression turns serious.

"Your journey isn't over yet, Sammy."

My heart starts to beat rapidly again. *He knows.*

"Everyone in Heaven has been praying for you."

A soft grin tugs at the corners of his mouth.

"Your new friend Joshua—wow, has he prayed. You should smell the fragrance of Heaven when he prays. It's been nonstop! He's a warrior for the Lord, and he cares for you deeply."

Stephen takes both of my hands in his.

"I need you to know: your life on Earth is not over. God has so much planned for you. Your life will have a ripple effect, Sammy. It matters."

His words confuse me and sting. Shame rises in my chest knowing Stephen knows my plan. *But maybe he doesn't know everything. Maybe he doesn't know about Mother and Father. He must think things are still good. That would explain why he's encouraging me to stay. But if he knew the truth—if he knew how bad it really is—there's no way he'd want me to stay there. He'd want me here. With him. With Jesus. I'll tell him everything. Then he'll understand.*

So I do.

I tell him about the last two years: Mother's yelling, the starving, the punishments. How she treats me like I'm the reason she's miserable. I explain how Father barely comes home, and when he does, it's like I don't exist.

I talk about the fights: the screaming, the slammed doors, the unbearable silence that follows.

I tell him how I lost all my friends. Mother made sure of that.

How the kids at school whisper behind my back or laugh in my face.

How isolated I feel.

I don't hold back. Not one detail. If he wants me to go back, he needs to understand what I'd be returning to.

I wait for him to say it's awful. That it's too much. I wait for him to say he understands now and maybe even that I should stay. But he doesn't.

Instead, he wraps me in a warm hug. He pulls back, pain in his eyes, and says gently, "Sammy, it hurts to hear how much you've had to suffer. I wish I could tell you what happens next, but that's not for any of us to know. What I do know is this: your story isn't over. There's still so much being written. Don't stop the ink."

I step back, stunned. *How could he say that? How could he hear everything I've been through and still tell me to go back?*

"You don't get it. It's like living in hell every single day. It's nothing like when you were alive."

I clench my hands into fists, trying to control the anger rising inside me.

"I believe now! I'll come to Heaven and be with you. We'll be happy!"

Stephen smiles, but it's a sad smile, not the reaction I was hoping for. My heart starts to sink.

"I'd love for you to join me in Heaven one day. But not on your own terms," he says softly.

"Until then, God's already at work in your story, Sammy. What's coming is better than you think. Please don't give up."

My shoulders slump in defeat. He doesn't understand. And it hurts.

I don't know how much longer I have with him, and I don't want to waste it talking about this. *I'll let it go for now. But one day he'll see. He'll understand.*

We walk through the meadow, talking and laughing. Stephen tells me all about life in Heaven. He tells me how everything he dreamed of doing on Earth is possible here.

His latest project is a bridge that stretches for miles, intricately built to look as if it's floating.

I smile.

He's become the engineer we always knew he could be.

He talks about how amazing it is to walk with God, just as it was always meant to be. To live in harmony with others, enjoying life as God created it.

It is Eden.

We are his children, and he is our Father. We never lack in Heaven.

I picture this as my new life—just me and Stephen—and that it would never end.

We finally approach the edge of the meadow, where trees begin to dot the horizon. Stephen turns to me, a look of peace crossing his face. I should feel reassured by the peace he carries, but instead I feel betrayed.

"Sammy, it's time to go back now. And you won't be coming here again tomorrow."

He hugs me tightly.

"I'm praying for you. I promise there's more to your life. You were made for something greater."

I start sobbing, the weight of goodbye hitting me all at once. I know I'll be back in my bed any moment.

"I don't want to leave you, Stephen. Please, just let me stay here with you!"

Anger flashes across my face. "If not now, then I'll be back in a few days!"

Stephen looks at me with sadness in his eyes. It breaks my heart that he's sad over what I need to do. But soon, we'll be reunited and it won't matter. *We'll be together again: me, Stephen, and Jesus. And we'll all be happy.*

Jesus comes walking out of the woods toward us. Stephen hugs me one final time and whispers, "I love you, Sammy. Please… don't give up." And then he's gone.

My heart sinks. I turn to Jesus. He's watching me carefully.

"Sammy, it's time for you to go back home," he says. "You've only seen a glimpse of glory. There is much more waiting for you in eternity."

He places a hand on my shoulder.

"When you return to Earth, seek me and you will find all that you've been searching for. All of Heaven is rooting for you, my dear Sammy. Don't give up."

He repeats the same words Stephen just spoke and it confuses me all the more. *They know how much pain I'm in. Why won't they just let me end it and come here where I could be free from pain? Don't they love me? Don't they want me to be happy?*

Jesus wraps his arms around me, and I soak in the peace and love that fill my heart.

I'll be back soon.

CHAPTER 14

"God is our refuge and strength,
a very present help in trouble."

PSALM 46:1 ESV

The trip through the tunnel lasts only a second.

My worst fear has come true. I'm back in my bed.

My eyes adjust to the dim light. Nothing has changed.

The wallpaper is still faded pink and peeling at the top.

My journal sits on the nightstand, untouched. No dust, no sign that time passed at all.

I let out a long sigh, my body numb.

A tear slips from my eye.

Oh, Stephen. I don't know how I'm supposed to do this life without you. I can't.

No matter what they say, there's still only one option. And it's getting closer.

I'll see you again soon.

A strange sense of relief fills my body, but it isn't like the joy I felt in Heaven. This is different. It makes me feel slightly sick, like when you eat too many sweets. In the moment, it feels good. But it leaves a lingering stomachache.

I dismiss the sick feeling, assuming it's just from not eating. I let myself relish the momentary "happiness," thinking about what's coming.

I close my eyes and drift into a blissful sleep. *I'll make it through these final days.*

. . .

My alarm goes off and I'm up in a flash, swinging my feet over the side of the bed. I start getting ready with a little more pep in my step than usual.

Maybe it's a side effect of going to Heaven two nights in a row, or maybe it's just that I no longer have to battle with my decision.

I do my hair a little differently today, tying it in a knot at the nape of my neck. It makes me look older, more put together. *Mother will be pleased with that.* I had ironed it carefully beforehand, making sure there wasn't a single wrinkle or spot left. My dress pants are pressed to perfection, not one crease out of place.

I look in the mirror and feel satisfied. Staring back at me is a girl who looks professional. Polished. Forced to grow up far beyond her years.

I'm determined to get through these last few days with ease, even if that means trying to appease my mother in every little thing I do.

A thump on my window makes me jump.

I walk over to investigate. Perched in the flower box is a hummingbird, blue and green. Just like the one I saw in Heaven.

It lays there motionless.

Bile rises in my throat.

It's dead.

I press my hand to my stomach and let out a stifled cry.

Shock rises, but I shove it back down where it belongs.

Slamming the curtains shut, I walk away.

This world is nothing but broken.

I hurry down the stairs, forcing the image of the dead humming-bird out of my mind.

I peek around the corner. *Perfect. I'm up before her.*

In the kitchen, I grab the eggs and start her favorite omelet.

I glance at the clock. *She'll be out any minute.*

This has to be timed just right.

Just as predicted, she walks through the kitchen door and sees me at the stove, dressed to her standard of perfection and making break-fast. She pauses in place, a dumbfounded look on her face.

"Good morning, Mother. I made you your favorite omelet. Would you like coffee and toast too?"

She stands there frozen. Most mornings I avoid her for as long as possible, only coming down at the last minute, hoping there's some-thing left for me to eat.

She finally snaps out of her stunned silence and walks to the table, still eyeing me with confusion.

"Yes, that will be fine," she says.

I bring her food to the table and pour her coffee into her favor-ite ceramic mug, two creams, one sugar cube. Just how she likes it.

I place it gently in front of her.

"I'm going to freshen up before the bus comes. It should be here in fifteen minutes. Have a good day," I say, excusing myself.

I climb the stairs quickly and stop in front of the mirror.

Smoothing back a few loose hairs and straightening my shirt, I nod to myself. *I'm ready.*

I head straight for the door. *No breakfast for me. I'm not about to push my luck. That exchange with Mother went well, and I'm not going to ruin it.*

Just as I'm about to open the door, Mother calls from the kitchen. "Samantha, come here!" I wince. *Just when I thought I was in the clear.*

I walk into the kitchen, bracing myself. But instead of yelling, Mother hands me an apple. She doesn't say anything, just returns to eating her breakfast. For the first time, she doesn't look at me. Her gaze stays fixed on her food.

"Thank you," is all I manage to say. I don't want to risk ruining the moment, so I quickly turn and walk out the door, biting into the apple before she can change her mind. I half-expect her to call me back and demand it in some cruel twist of power.

She doesn't, and I finish the apple before I reach the bus. I toss the core into the bushes, my stomach just full enough to keep the hunger quiet.

Stepping onto the bus with a little more energy than usual, I offer a quiet "hi" to a few of the kids who are already staring. Their eyes are full of hate, and for the first time, I wonder if maybe they have rough lives at home too, if they're carrying pain and just don't know what to do with it.

I sit in my familiar seat at the back of the bus, staring out the window, watching two raindrops race to the bottom of the glass. The sun tries to peek through the drizzle.

I close my eyes and imagine I'm back in Heaven with Stephen and Jesus.

Maybe that's why I've seen Joshua do the same thing.

Behind his closed eyes, is he back in the Amazon? Feeling free and untamed? Exploring with no fear?

Thinking of Joshua, I feel a flicker of excitement. *I can't wait to tell him about my latest adventure. But I also have questions, ones I need answers to. Like why he chooses to stay in this painful world. Why, if he's seen what I've seen, doesn't he just end his life too and go back to Heaven?*

We finally pull up to Joshua's house, and he's standing outside with his hood pulled low over his eyes. He walks onto the bus, still clutching his Bible like usual, but I notice a slight tremble in his hands. He makes his way to the back and sits down next to me. When he turns to face me, I see what he's been hiding beneath the hood. His right eye is nearly swollen shut, and a cut stretches just below it.

I gasp, "Joshua, what happened?"

He tries to smile but the wounds are too fresh, and his attempt at smiling only causes them to split further. His jaw tightens.

"Dad's drinking again," he says quietly. "My mom left for work early, like she always does. As soon as she left, instead of going to his job, my dad started drinking."

He clenches his fists. "That's why we had to move from California. He showed up to work drunk and got fired."

His voice starts to shake. "My mom's sister lives in Maine. She offered us a fresh start. He'd been sober for two weeks... said he'd never touch it again."

A tear falls from the eye that isn't swollen.

"I got so mad when I saw him sitting on the couch with a half-empty bottle of vodka," he says through gritted teeth. "I yelled at him. Told him he promised."

He gestures to the swelling and the cut. "And this is what I got."

I flinch, my heart aching for him.

"I had to come to school," he continues. "If I didn't, my mom would've found out. And we're already barely getting by. They don't say it, but I can tell by the cans of soup we live off of. If she had to leave work for me, we couldn't afford it."

His shoulders slump, and for the first time, I see defeat in his posture. His eyes close for a moment, and his palms open, facing upward, like when he prayed yesterday.

His lips move silently.

Slowly, the pain on his face begins to lift. It's replaced by something I'm still trying to understand: *peace.*

When his eyes open again, I speak.

"I can't believe your dad did that. I'm sorry, Joshua. It's not fair. You don't deserve that."

I take his hand and give it a soft squeeze. I want to say more, but I don't know where to start.

Joshua's next words catch me off guard.

"I forgive him, Sammy."

He looks into my eyes with quiet conviction.

"I know what he did isn't right, but I've tried holding onto anger before…" His voice trails off, pain flashing across his face. "It nearly cost me my life."

There's more to his story, more than he's saying, but I can't focus on that right now. My blood boils with anger.

"How can you forgive someone who's hurt you like this? I don't think God expects us to forgive abusers!"

Joshua smiles gently. Peace spreads across his face. The pain I saw earlier is completely gone.

"I know… it doesn't always make sense to me either. But the truth is no one's perfect. Some sins carry louder consequences, but we've all fallen short. God has forgiven me, and with his help, I'll forgive those who've hurt me."

He squeezes my hand. I didn't even realize I was still holding his.

"And besides, holding onto bitterness and anger doesn't punish them. It punishes me. I won't let it consume me again."

I shake my head, anger rising on his behalf.

Well, I could never forgive the people who've hurt me. They don't deserve it.

Joshua notices the flash of anger on my face. Somehow, he always knows when I'm not ready to budge.

"Alright, Sammy," he says gently. "Let's talk about something else. How about the adventure you went on last night?"

He winks at me, then leans his head back on the seat, a soft grin tugging at his lips.

"How do you always know what's going on?" I ask, frustration lacing my voice. The anger from earlier still simmers, unwilling to let me go.

"Let's just say me and God are close," he says with another wink.

I can't help but smile.

Maybe it's time I stopped trying to figure it all out. After the past few days, the impossible feels almost... normal.

"You could know too, if you just asked." He nudges my shoulder, lightening the mood.

I start to relax, the anger finally loosening its grip. It's nearly impossible to stay upset around Joshua. *I may never understand everything, but maybe that's okay.*

I begin to share, my voice rising with excitement as I tell him about Stephen, about Jesus, and the meadow. I tell him how Stephen urged me not to give up and how Joshua's prayers had echoed through all of Heaven.

Joshua beams, his eyes clear and bright, no trace of the pain that clouded them earlier. I still don't understand how he can carry such peace while walking through so much suffering.

"That's amazing, Sammy. I can't believe you got to see Stephen. What a gift. God is so kind."

His eyes shine, catching the morning light.

"Did it help? After everything they said, are you going to stay? Because it sounds like God has something pretty incredible planned for you here."

My heart drops. *Another person asking me to stay here in the pain, and I still don't understand why.*

"I don't get it. Why is everyone asking me to stay here in pain when I could be free? It doesn't make sense."

A sudden thought rushes to the surface.

"Why don't you come with me, Joshua? We'll go together, and then we'll both be free!"

I've been speaking quickly, excitement rising in my chest as I stare out the window. But when I finally turn back to Joshua, I freeze.

Tears are streaming down his face.

"What's wrong, Joshua? Does your eye hurt?"

Without hesitation, he wraps his arm around me and pulls me into a tight hug.

"I'm sorry that life has been so cruel to you that you think this is the only way. I wish you could see how amazing you are and how your life will make an impact. It already has… on me. You were created for a purpose."

He lets out a sigh, and I lean into the warmth of his hug, feeling a sense of security I don't want to let go of just yet.

"I thought that if you saw Heaven, if you saw how real Jesus is and that he died so you could live, if you glimpsed the glory that's waiting for you one day, it would give you the strength to keep going here. To discover the plans God has for you now. You're needed here, Sammy. Please, don't give up. I know life will get better."

He pulls away just as the bus stops in front of the school. I step off in silence.

Joshua's words echo in my head, looping over and over, leaving me more confused than ever, just like I felt last night after leaving Stephen and Jesus.

They don't understand. Or am I the one missing something?

CHAPTER 15

*"For I consider that the sufferings of this
present time are not worth comparing with
the glory that is to be revealed to us."*

ROMANS 8:18 ESV

I watch the clock on the wall.

A minute drags by.

It's strange to think that, in a way, it's a countdown to the end.

The teacher drones on about atoms, but it's just background noise now.

My thoughts won't stop, bouncing between memories and conversations from the past forty-eight hours.

Sometimes, they drift further… to dreams I had as a kid: becoming a journalist, traveling the world, maybe even getting married someday.

They say life is worth living.

Are they right?

But how long would it take? I'd still have to survive my mother and father for at least a couple more years. Would I make it that long? I'm not sure.

What was it that Jesus said to me?

When you get back, seek me, and you'll find what you're looking for.

Now, what does that mean?

I let the thought trail off. It's almost lunchtime, and I'm hoping to eat with Joshua again. As much as I should avoid him, I can't. There's a pull, a kinship I've never felt before, not even with my childhood best friends.

Those friendships feel shallow now after knowing Joshua.

He sees me.

He accepts me.

The bell rings, and I grab my books and rush down the hallway.

I spot Megan and her crew up ahead.

I inwardly groan.

I try to avoid them at all costs, especially in the hallway, where there's less teacher supervision.

Megan is whispering to the new girl, Heather.

She seemed nice when she first arrived, but the vultures quickly claimed her.

Whatever Megan's saying, it's making Heather uncomfortable. She glances from me to the floor and back again.

This can't be good.

The girls spread out across the hallway, blocking my path.

I glance around, hoping to see a teacher.

Other students pause, watching with interest. A few snicker. Some pull out their phones.

My heart starts to pound.

Megan nudges Heather forward.

Heather hesitates, looking around anxiously. But when she catches Megan's expression, she gives in.

She starts toward me. For a moment, it looks like she'll pass right by, but then her shoulder slams into mine.

I grip my books to keep them from falling.

Laughter erupts around us.

Heather casts me a glance—part apology, part regret—and falls back in line beside Megan.

Annoyed that the stunt didn't get a bigger reaction, Megan struts over and slaps the books from my hands.

They scatter across the floor.

I stand frozen, refusing to bend down and give her the satisfaction.

"What are you going to do, Sammy? Go cry to your brother?" Megan sneers.

"Oh wait… he's dead."

My eyes fill with tears before I can stop them.

Victory flashes across her face.

Heather looks horrified.

The other girls laugh, but their smiles falter.

The hallway goes quiet.

I need to get out of here, but I can't move.

That's when I feel a gentle hand on my back.

Joshua is standing next to me.

He takes one look at my pale face, my eyes brimming with tears, and his expression darkens.

He steps forward, placing himself between me and Megan.

She has to tilt her head up to meet his eyes, but she doesn't back down.

He doesn't yell. He speaks calmly and clearly.

"You keep choosing to be mean. But that doesn't make you strong, it makes you weak."

Silence. They stand there face to face, not breaking away.

His swollen eye and the cut beneath it make his stare even more intense.

I'm suddenly glad I'm not on the receiving end of that look.

Then, without another word, he bends down, gathers my books, and gently places an arm around my shoulders.

He walks us through the crowd.

Megan, not used to being dismissed, yells after us,

"Perfect, now there's two weirdos! You guys make the cutest couple! Watch where you're walking next time, unless you like getting another bruised face!"

Joshua ignores the last comment and smiles.

My face flushes pink.

"She can't go five minutes without thinking about us," he says with a grin. "It's kind of sweet."

A few kids laugh.

Some glance at Megan, eyebrows raised.

For once, she doesn't have a comeback.

We thankfully make our way into the cafeteria, my face refusing to return to its normal shade. Joshua drops his arm as we walk through the door, realizing I'm uncomfortable. He eyes me cautiously, but I refuse to make eye contact.

Without saying anything, I break away and head toward the lunch line. I need a couple of moments to myself. *I can't believe he stood up for me. He wasn't even afraid.*

I blush, thinking about Megan calling us a couple. *Did he think that too? I've only known him for two days. He's kind of cute, and really sweet, but I can't be thinking like this. My time here is almost over.*

I glance toward the door and spot Joshua waiting. He waves and then walks outside, heading toward our spot.

I quickly grab some pasta, pay for it, and walk toward the exit. We really are nobodies. No one even notices the two of us sneaking out every day. Even after the hallway incident, no one gives me a second glance as I slip through the door.

The sun hits my face. The warmth is a nice surprise. Crossing the damp grass, I spot Joshua lying on a blanket under the tree. He must've brought it with him. I was too flustered in the hallway to notice.

My stomach tightens, anxiety creeping in after everything that happened in the hallway. But I need to talk to him. I force myself forward, trying to muster up some of the courage I saw in him.

As I get closer, I hear Joshua singing. *"God, I praise you. You are holy, you are worthy."* The words float through the air like a gentle breeze. My skin tingles, and the air feels electric.

My jaw drops. I freeze in place, caught between fear and awe. Standing next to Joshua is an angel. He looks like Marie, but with masculine features, strong and radiant. Joshua doesn't seem to notice him.

My eyes catch movement above. The sky begins to split open. And then I see them. An assembly of angels fills the sky, their voices echoing Joshua's song. And in the center of them is Jesus.

I drop my food. My eyes burn from the brilliance above, unable to look directly at the glory before me. I shield my face and blink, trying to make it go away. Maybe I'm hallucinating. Then I hear Joshua's laughter.

He sees it too.

Without meaning to, I join in. I can't help it. Joy fills the air like sunlight warming the earth, and I laugh until I can't catch my breath.

Suddenly, the sky closes.

I run to Joshua, collapsing beside him on the blanket, breathless, wide-eyed, still reeling from what just happened.

"What... what was that?" I whisper.

Joshua sits up, grinning from ear to ear. "Well, my friend, that's what I'd call another glimpse of glory."

He chuckles, brushing his hands off. "I was lying here, worshiping God, thinking about my dad this morning, our conversation on the bus, the hallway drama… it was a lot. I was struggling. But God heard me."

His face lights up, full of gratitude. "And he opened our eyes and gave us another glimpse of glory. This world feels heavy sometimes, but there's so much happening that we can't see. There's a battle between light and darkness and today, we got to see the light."

He turns to me, his voice softer now. "We got to see our friend. My reason for living. My hope."

Tears trickle from his eyes, his face once again shining bright with peace. He turns his head toward me, his brown eyes glowing in the sunlight.

He clears his throat. "You asked me why I don't just end my life, and the truth is, I did try."

He looks up at the sky, tears slipping down his cheeks.

"I wasn't always a believer. My mom was. She dragged me and my dad to church for most of my life. I thought it was all make-believe—just a tool to control people."

He lets out a short chuckle. "Boy, was I wrong."

His face grows somber. "A year ago, things got really bad with my dad's drinking. He and my mom were always yelling. She tried to shield me, to keep the peace. One night, she was working late, and I was home alone with him. I didn't realize he'd been drinking again. I just wanted to go to the movies with some friends. I went downstairs and asked if I could go."

His voice falters. "He snapped. Pushed me down and started yelling, 'You can't hurt me! You can't hurt me!' Like he didn't even know who I was. I kept yelling that it was me, but he was gone, like in a trance. He had a cigar in his mouth, and it fell in the struggle… gave me that scar you saw on my arm."

He swipes at a tear. "I was terrified. I broke free and ran upstairs, locked my door. I could hear him pounding on it, crying, saying he was sorry. Begging to be let in."

He lets out a shaky breath. "I was just… done. So tired of it all. In that moment, I did something to try to take the pain away. I didn't want to live anymore. My mom found me fifteen minutes later. She told me later that, while working, she suddenly felt a searing pain across her wrists and then heard a voice say, 'Get home. Now.'"

Tears roll down my face. I squeeze his arm, letting him know I'm here.

He continues softly, "As I lay in the hospital bed, barely alive, I saw him. I saw Jesus. He held his hands over my wrists. I could see the healed holes in his. That's when I knew he was real. He died for me. And he was saving me."

His voice trembles. "I told him I was sorry. I told him I wanted to live. The doctors told my mom that if she'd arrived even a minute later, I wouldn't have made it. They said it was a miracle that the bleeding was slower than it should have been, but I knew why. Jesus was holding my wrists."

He shakes his head. "No one believed me, except my mom. She wept and prayed with me. That was the beginning of my relationship with Jesus."

He pauses, eyes glistening. "It hasn't been easy. Some days are still really hard. But shortly after the hospital stay, I went to Heaven. That's when the adventures with Jesus began. He didn't have to do that, but he did. Because he loves us."

Joshua looks right at me, voice steady now. "When life gets heavy, I remember what the Bible says: 'For I know the plans I have for you… plans for hope and a future.' And I keep going. God has a purpose for me here. And until he takes me home, I'm going to fulfill that purpose, no matter the cost. So yes, I've tried to end my life. But I've seen a glimpse of eternity. And now, my heart is sold out to proclaim who he is until my very last day."

I stare at Joshua, stunned by what he just shared. "Wow… I didn't know," I whisper, guilt tightening in my chest. "I'm so sorry, Joshua. I just… I don't think I'm as strong as you."

Joshua looks at me intently. "Sammy, it's not about who's the strongest, believe me. Most days, I don't feel strong at all. But I cry out to God, and look at what he does. He shows up. He always will."

I don't know what else to say.

Joshua had tried to take his life.

Feeling suddenly uneasy with how deep the conversation has gone, I shift gears.

"I never thanked you, for earlier. In the hallway. No one's ever stood up for me like that."

Joshua seems slightly relieved at the change of subject, the pain slowly fading from his face.

"I'll always stand up for you, Sammy. You're my friend."

He chuckles, and just the sound of it lightens the mood.

"I was actually really nervous in the hallway. I was praying the whole time. Girl bullies freak me out."

He laughs again, but this one carries a hint of sadness.

"I've dealt with my fair share of bullies. Over time, I learned to pray for them. Something made them that way. I don't envy them, I pity them."

I open my mouth to bring up the "couple" comment, even though I really don't want to. But before I can, Joshua cuts in.

"And by the way, I'm happy to be just friends."

I relax. *He gets it.*

I glance up at the sky. "Is this what you see every day?"

Joshua looks up too, a smile filling his face.

"God is a good Father—something neither of us has really experienced. But he's always giving us gifts. Sometimes it's not so tangible, maybe just a peace that fills my heart, or an encouraging message, or meeting a new friend."

He nudges my side and grins.

"All we have to do is open our eyes and our hearts. He's always speaking, always trying to show us that he's with us."

"DON'T LISTEN TO HIM."

A dominating voice fills my mind so loud it drowns out everything else. It's the only voice I can hear.

"I think it's just too late for me, Joshua," I say quietly. "I've already made up my mind. It's just easier this way."

I look down.

"I didn't expect to meet a friend these last few days. And because of you, I got to see Heaven, meet Jesus, and see Stephen again."

I manage a small smile.

"Your prayers showed me the truth. And because of that, I have enough peace to get through what's ahead."

I pause, the weight of my words sinking in.

"I'm ready to go."

Joshua looks away, wiping at his eyes. The tears don't stop.

"Sammy, I'm going to keep praying you change your mind."

He stands suddenly, urgency in his movements. Looking down at me one last time, he says, "You're needed here, Sammy."

Then he walks away, leaving me sitting there alone with all my thoughts.

Especially the loud ones.

"YOU'RE MAKING THE RIGHT DECISION."

Then why do I feel sick?

Why can't I see what Joshua is talking about?

I pick up the blanket along with my books Joshua had been carrying for me. I decide to return the blanket to the nurse's office; he must've borrowed it from there.

I take a different route than usual, hoping to avoid Megan and her crew. The hallway is unfamiliar, which is odd since our school isn't that big.

That's when something on the wall catches my eye.

I stop. The blanket drops from my hands.

On the sign, in big bold letters:

YOU'RE NEEDED HERE.

Underneath, the suicide hotline.

CHAPTER 16

*"Then you will call upon me and come and pray
to me, and I will hear you. You will seek me and
find me, when you seek me with all your heart."*

JEREMIAH 29:12-13 ESV

The air has turned chilly as I walk along the cracked sidewalks. Weeds push through the pavement, invasive like my thoughts.

I couldn't bring myself to go to my tutoring session.

It's a long walk home, but I need the time to think.

The weight of the sign lingers in my mind.

Did Joshua put it there?

How would he know I'd walk down that one specific hallway?

I've never seen a sign like that at school before.

I slow my steps and pull my phone from my backpack.

It's not a smartphone; it's just for calls and texts.

My mother doesn't want me "distracted" by social media, or the internet at all.

The number from the poster is seared into my brain.

Only three numbers.

9-8-8.

What if I called it?

Maybe I should start listening to what everyone is saying.

I almost chicken out. I start to put the phone away.

But then—

A wave of courage rushes through me.

My heart races as I shakily type in the numbers, my fingers moving even though I'm terrified.

I hover over the call button.

Here we go. I'm going to make the call—

I freeze.

My phone's vibrating.

Incoming call... Mother.

I have about five seconds to decide what to do.

I can hit ignore and face the wrath later and call the hotline.

Or I can answer, get it over with, and then call the hotline after.

I choose the latter.

"Hi, Mother."

I hold the phone away from my ear as her screams pierce through the line.

"Where are you? Your tutor just called and said you never showed up! You better have a good explanation!"

The shaking returns. I clear my throat, trying to keep my emotions in check. "I'm sorry. I wasn't feeling well." It's only a half-lie. "I thought some fresh air might help, so I walked. I'll be home soon."

"I can't deal with this anymore, your constant lying and disobedience! Your father can deal with you this time."

The phone goes silent. I take it away from my ear, trembling.

My father's home?

The last time he was home was a month ago, on my birthday. I remember feeling so excited that he remembered. I sat on the edge of the couch, all dressed up.

He walked in, barely lifting his eyes from his phone. He made brief eye contact and muttered "hi" before making a call. He was gone within fifteen minutes. He only came to grab more clothes.

I quicken my pace. The longer I take, the angrier they'll be.

The hotline already feels like a distant memory.

I round the corner where Pine Street meets Front Street. His Mercedes is already in the driveway. My stomach sinks.

I take a deep breath, trying to calm my nerves.

I was hoping I wouldn't have to see him before I carried out my plan, but I guess I don't have a choice.

Here we go.

I walk into the house. He's sitting in the living room, the newspaper propped up in his hands. I don't see my mother anywhere.

A one-on-one chat with my father is never good.

"Hello, Samantha," he says casually, like this is something we do every day. *His voice is calm. Too calm.*

I close the door behind me and whisper a shaky, "Hi."

His hair is speckled with more gray than the last time I saw him, and he looks tired, like these last two years have caught up to him all at once.

"Sit down, Samantha." He gestures toward the loveseat across from his recliner.

I'm not ready for another scolding—especially not from a parent who's barely in my life.

I wish he would just stay away until I could do what I needed to do.

But… is my mind changing? I almost called the hotline today.

I stifle a scoff.

This is exactly why I'm glad I didn't call. They wouldn't be able to help me.

I sit on the opposite couch, fidgeting with my hands until I notice my father's brooding eyes fixed on me.

"I thought everything was under control here, but your mother says you skipped your tutoring session even though you're already struggling in algebra. And on top of that, you've been lying to her. We don't tolerate lying in this house. What's going on?"

I nervously look him in the eye, gathering every ounce of courage I have, and try to explain.

"I felt sick today after school. I've been trying my best lately, though. I got an eighty-nine on an algebra test today. I think I'll be able to bring my grade up to a B-plus by the end of the semester. I thought I was doing better, so missing one tutoring session didn't seem like a big deal."

My father shakes his head.

"That's not good enough. Do you really want to end up at a community college? Because with your current grades, that's all you'll get into. We've talked about this. You need to try harder."

I can see the anger brewing behind his dark green eyes. The same eyes that used to shine with love and pride now look ice cold. I feel myself shrinking, sinking deeper into the couch.

"Next time, don't assume you know what's best. We're the parents."

He sighs, clearly frustrated. "I work hard so you can have a good life, but maybe it's time I cut back and stay home more. Your mother clearly can't handle you on her own and I won't watch you fail. We don't fail in this family."

My mother walks into the living room at that moment, a frustrated look on her face. For just a second, I see a flash of sadness in her eyes. Sometimes I forget that I didn't just lose my father when Stephen died. She lost her husband. I almost pity her. But the feeling vanishes quickly as I remember how cruel she's been to me.

The evening plays out exactly how I expected once I saw Father was home.

I get to eat dinner because he likes to pretend we're a normal, loving family.

He knows she withholds food. I've begged him to talk to her, to tell her to stop.

But one dark look from him and I never brought it up again.

He's only grown more distant over time.

He used to be gentle. Patient. The kind of dad who tucked me in and kissed my forehead.

But something changed.

A darkness built up in him, slow and quiet.

Now, anger flashes out in seconds, and there have been moments where I've come close to experiencing what Joshua has.

I never thought he was capable of that.

But now, I don't dare test him.

I try to be on my best behavior, silently praying that the Jesus I met in Heaven will protect me.

"You're never home! What do you expect me to do? I work too!" Mother screams, her face beet red, eyes wild with rage.

Father slams his fist on the table.

"Enough!"

I sit up straighter, staring at my almost-empty plate.

My hands shake in my lap.

My parents can't make it through a single meal without fighting.

I'm finally dismissed to my room early and I don't hesitate.

I wash my dish and load it into the dishwasher.

They sit at the table, seething at each other in silence.

Once I'm in my room and the door is shut, they resume.

For the rest of the evening, I listen to them scream.

Most of it is about me.

About how Father is never home.

How Mother is left to do all the parenting alone.

Every now and then, I hear a loud thud—

probably something Mother threw at him.

I'll get to clean it up in the morning.

They hide behind their reputations, work, image, charity events. But behind closed doors, they're entirely different people. If only the world could see through the facade.

This could last for hours, so I throw my pillow over my ears and picture Heaven. I picture walking with Jesus, hearing his laugh, feeling his joy and peace again. I think about Stephen and running with him through the meadow.

Soon, I remind myself, *very soon, I'll be with them.*

* * *

I feel overwhelmed from the day and pull out my journal, hoping it will help ease some of the confusion I'm feeling.

This time, I don't address the universe.

I want to talk to the only one I know is real.

Dear God,

Today was exhausting. I can't believe what Joshua's dad did to him. Do you really want us to forgive people who physically hurt us? It doesn't seem fair. That man made Joshua want to die. He actually tried. But he still wants to live? There was a suicide hotline poster at school. I've never seen it before. Did you put it there? Are you trying to tell me something? And what about my parents? You heard them tonight, right? You really can't expect me to stay. Please… can someone just understand? I just don't want to feel like nobody loves me anymore.

Sincerely lost & confused,
Sammy

I don't feel any better. I glance at the clock—only nine. Too early to try and force myself to sleep.

A once-forbidden thought drifts into my mind:

Maybe I should read my Bible.

I remember the little white Bible my grandma gave me when I was five. My grandparents were devoted Christians, but they passed away shortly after that birthday, before they could leave much of an impression on my life. Still, I remember always feeling warm and safe around them. The same way I felt in Heaven. The same way I feel around Joshua.

Images of Joshua flood my mind: his contagious smile, joyous even in the middle of pain. His face filled with sadness when I told him I'd made up my mind. *I don't want to be the reason that smile disappears.*

I rummage through the boxes in my closet, unsure where I put the Bible. I was never interested in reading it before. Old school projects and pictures from a time when our family felt whole spill out.

I pick up a drawing I made in first grade and trace my fingers over the stick-figure family, all of them smiling. I find myself smiling too, until a single tear drops onto the page, distorting my little stick-figure face. *How fitting.*

Finally, at the bottom of a box filled with books, I find it. *My little white Bible.*

I pick it up, the delicate white cover feeling fragile in my hands. I carry it over to my bed and sit down, unsure where to begin, but something stirs in my heart, telling me this is exactly what I need right now.

There's a bookmark tucked inside. It opens to Psalms.

I've heard of Psalms. Whenever we went to church, the service always started with one, so it feels like a good place to start.

I flip to Psalm 23 and begin to read:

"The Lord is my shepherd; I shall not want.
He makes me lie down in green pastures.
He leads me beside still waters.
He restores my soul.
He leads me in paths of righteousness for his name's sake.
Even though I walk through the valley of the shadow of death,
I will fear no evil, for you are with me;
your rod and your staff, they comfort me.
You prepare a table before me in the presence of my enemies;
you anoint my head with oil; my cup overflows.
Surely goodness and mercy shall follow me
all the days of my life,
and I shall dwell in the house of the Lord forever."

I close the Bible slowly as tears spill onto the cover.

A peace settles over me deeper than anything I've ever felt. The kind that can only come from being in Jesus' presence.

No book has ever made me feel this way before.

The words felt alive, as if they reached into my heart and lit something up.

Surely goodness and mercy shall follow me all the days of my life.

The verse echoes in my mind as I curl up under the blanket.

My body relaxes.

My soul feels… still.

I don't go to Heaven tonight.

Instead, I dream of green pastures and still waters.

CHAPTER 17

My hand hovers over the calendar. The red marker trembles in my grip. I set it down on the nightstand, unable to mark the next X.

It's Friday. My last day of school—ever.

A mixture of emotions churns inside me.

Relief, because it's the last time I'll have to face my bullies.

And sadness, because it's the last time I'll see Joshua.

If Joshua had come to our school sooner, would everything be different? It makes me question if I really want to leave. So soon, anyway.

In a couple of years, I would be eighteen and heading to college, if I got a scholarship. I wouldn't have to rely on my parents anymore. That would mean freedom, especially if I went to college far away.

But I'd need to get my grades up. I've let them slip slightly, thinking it wouldn't matter. But maybe… it still could. If I started today and focused, if I attended every tutoring session and poured myself into my schoolwork for the next three years, maybe that would ensure my freedom.

Mrs. Rhine thought I could be a journalist. She believed in me before I even believed in myself. She even submitted my name for that college course. *Could I still take it?*

Could I really do this… live?

There might even be ways for me to find relief in my life, right now. Joshua told me about a new church he and his mom started going to. He invited me to come with him this Sunday. He said there's a youth group, and the kids are actually nice.

Joshua said they're different. They accepted him for who he is. He thinks I'd like them.

Would my mother let me attend? Normally, she spends her entire Sunday locked in her room, only coming out to eat. She typically leaves me alone that day. It would look good on the family if I attended church. Bonus points, since my mother and father stopped attending regularly a long time ago.

I was sure of the end. But Heaven, Jesus, Stephen—and Joshua— shattered that certainty. The peace I once had about ending things is now getting all mixed up. The thought is starting to make me feel uneasy.

I'm not sure I can go through with it anymore.

There is a chance my life could get better and I'm not sure I'm ready to give that up. Especially with someone like Joshua in my life.

I grab my journal and sit on the edge of my bed.

Flipping it open, I write the only words I can manage.

Two more days?

I drop my pen when I catch sight of the time. I need to hurry and get ready. I heard my father leave the house late last night. The slamming of the door and the car starting was a dead giveaway. At least I won't have to deal with him and my mother this morning.

It's hard enough to feel the hate from my mother, but to also feel it from my father, who I used to look up to so much, is beyond heartbreaking.

The loss of a father's love is one of the most devastating things that can happen to a young girl's heart.

I carefully come downstairs, unsure of what mood my mother will be in after fighting all night with my father. The sight before me is not what I'm expecting, and it leaves me feeling shocked.

My mother is sitting at the table, tears streaming down her face, staring into a full cup of coffee. There's no longer any steam coming from it. She looks vulnerable. Nothing like the harsh woman she has become over these years.

I feel incredibly awkward to have caught her in such a raw moment, especially knowing how she feels about showing weakness. I'm not sure how to respond.

Should I go back upstairs and wait until it's time to leave for school? I'll probably face her wrath if she catches me watching her in such an emotional state.

Before I can turn around and run, Mother senses my presence, lifts her head, and catches me standing in the doorway in stunned silence.

Her eyes are swollen and red from crying, and she looks like she hasn't slept all night.

Her voice cracks as she speaks, clearly shocked to see me there. "Sa-mantha, what are you doing down here so early?"

Wishing I had waited upstairs and avoided this awkward exchange, I slowly walk into the kitchen and stand in front of the table, my hands anxiously holding onto the back of a chair.

"It's almost time for school. This is always the time I come downstairs."

Mother turns and looks at the clock on the oven and shakes her head.

"I didn't realize it was that late. I must have been sitting here for quite a while."

She sighs, pushing her cold mug of coffee away from her.

"Samantha, start a fresh pot of coffee and put some bread in the toaster: one for me, one for you. Then come sit down."

I walk over hesitantly to the coffee pot and get it going, bewildered by the fact that my mother is asking me to join her for breakfast.

The coffee brews painfully slow, and the toast pops up out of the toaster, making me jump as I'm lost in thought.

I put strawberry jam on my mother's toast and choose apricot for mine. It's my favorite and I haven't had it in weeks.

The coffee maker beeps, cutting through the stillness.

I pour a cup of coffee for my mother and sit down at the table, avoiding eye contact in case she realizes what she's allowing me to do and puts an end to it.

We eat in silence for a while.

I glance up every so often to catch a glimpse of this woman who has replaced my mother. She looks defeated sitting there, and my heart suddenly aches for her.

Lord, I know she hasn't treated me well these past two years, but help her.

The short prayer fills my mind before I can stop it. It feels odd for me to pray, but lately, things have been changing in my heart. I'm seeing things differently, and I can feel my heart softening.

"Samantha, there's something I need to tell you."

I finally look up at her. Her knuckles are turning white around the mug. My stomach starts to sink.

She takes a deep, shaky breath, her mouth trembling.

"Your father has been having an affair."

She chokes up, then clears her throat.

"For the past year."

She goes on to tell me that the late nights staying at the office and the business trips away were all just a cover-up. That was just the story she clung to so she wouldn't have to face the truth. A way to save herself from embarrassment.

They're getting a divorce.

I don't say a word. I don't know what to say.

I'm processing all the emotions at once:

Hurt beyond belief.

Anger seething toward the man who abandoned not only his daughter, but now his marriage and family, too.

And somehow, also… relief.

Relief that I finally know the truth.

It finalizes my suspicions that my father truly does not care about me anymore.

Once again, my decision becomes easy.

I will be gone soon.

This can be a fresh start for my mother.

She will be by herself and can move on and maybe find happiness in this miserable world.

I don't know what to possibly say.

Does she deserve any condolences from me?

No, probably not.

But seeing her broken, human for once, I tell her I'm sorry that he did that to her. And then I harden my heart and that is the end of the conversation.

I clean up the kitchen in a robotic manner and say goodbye to my mother, who is still sitting at the table with her head in her hands, not saying goodbye in return.

She is a shell of a human, so far from the mother I once knew.

I walk out to the bus stop, once again feeling my world shift.

God, how could you keep letting this happen?

Haven't I dealt with enough?

I lost my brother, my mother went crazy, and my father—who was already an angry jerk—is now moving on with his mistress.

I've made up my mind, and this time, I'm not changing it.

Soon, I'll be gone, and so will the pain.

CHAPTER 18

"Jesus said to her, "I am the resurrection and the
life. Whoever believes in me, though he die, yet
shall he live, and everyone who lives and believes
in me shall never die. Do you believe this?"

JOHN 11:25-26 ESV

I get onto the bus like I have almost every morning for the last eight years, and as I look around at the worn brown seats filled with kids I have grown up with, the realization slowly hits me that this is the last time I will be riding the bus.

I wonder if anyone will notice when I don't get on the bus Monday morning. Will they even care?

It feels ceremonial as I walk down the narrow aisle, the last time I will feel the beady eyes of hatred or hear the whispers that make my skin flush. I see Jenny and Jessica just two rows ahead of where I am. There's an empty seat next to them, and for some reason, I feel compelled to sit with them. After all, I'm leaving, so who cares what I do at this point?

My fear is gone.

Jesus, help me to make a connection with them today. I hate to end it this way with two people who used to mean so much to me.

I take a deep breath as I stop at their seats. They both look up at me. Time freezes for a moment.

"Hey—"

The bus jolts forward. I lose my balance for a second and grab the seat next to me to steady myself.

"Sit down!" the bus driver yells. My courage falters.

I look at Jenny and Jessica one more time, then quickly hurry to the back of the bus. I plop down on the brown seat with the rip in the back. Its broken-in cushion welcomes me.

Jenny peers around her seat, a look of confusion crossing her face as she meets my eyes. For a moment, it looks like she might get up, but Jessica says something to her, and she turns away.

They're better off without me. It's for the best that we don't say goodbye.

The bus rolls down the street. I lean my forehead against the cold window. The tree-lined roads blur past, their green leaves brighter than usual glowing against the foggy backdrop.

A mother and her daughter walk hand in hand on the sidewalk. The little girl points at a patch of flowers, stopping to pick one. She hands it to her mom, who smiles and holds it like it's her most cherished treasure.

A tear slips down my cheek.

Mom, I miss you.

I wipe it away. We'll be at Joshua's house soon.

I force a smile across my lips.

Maybe I can let him believe I've decided to stay.

We can have a final day full of happy memories.

As we approach his house, the driver slows down. I quickly scan the yard, searching for him, but he isn't outside.

The bus keeps rolling, and my stomach drops.

An image of the creature from my room flashes before my eyes.

I squeeze them shut, fear coursing through my veins.

When I open them, there's nothing there.

Just a brown seat in front of me, with the same old piece of gum stuck to the back. It's been there for as long as I can remember.

It's probably nothing, I tell myself. *Maybe he walked again. He'll be waiting at school, leaning against a wall, eyes closed, Bible in hand.*

But the pit in my stomach doesn't ease.

I arrive at the school and get off the bus as quickly as I can. Of course, being in the back, I have to wait behind all the other kids who have no reason to rush off like I do.

Once I finally get off, I scan the schoolyard, searching for him.

I rush to the side of the building, to his usual spot.

He's not there.

Maybe he's already inside.

The sinking feeling in my stomach grows and finds its way into my chest.

I can't breathe. *Something is wrong. I feel it in my bones.*

I force myself to go into my first class. I nervously tap my pencil against my desk, watching the clock.

Mrs. Rhine is going over the assignment, but I'm too distracted. I need to get to lunch and find Joshua.

The intercom static breaks through my thoughts.

Mrs. Rhine stops talking and signals for us to pay attention to the speaker.

Mr. Brown clears his throat, and then his deep voice solemnly speaks.

"Good morning. There's no easy way to say this, and it's with a heavy heart that I share some difficult news. Our newest student, Joshua Littleton, has passed away. At this time, no further details are available. Please keep his family and friends in your thoughts and prayers. Grief counselors will be available throughout the day. If you need support, you may leave your classroom at any time. Just let your teacher know and head to the auditorium."

The room goes silent.

The air turns thick. I can't breathe.

I drop my head to the desk as the darkness creeps in from the edges of my vision.

Breathe, Sam. Just breathe.

I take a few shaky inhales, trying to steady myself.

Tears slip down my cheeks.

A few kids glance my way.

They've seen us together. They know.

Mrs. Rhine sees me with my head down and comes up to me.

"Sam, why don't you go down to the nurse's office and lay down for a little bit? Then maybe you can meet with one of the grief counselors. I'm so sorry about your friend, Joshua."

Tears fill her eyes, and I just want to fall into her arms and cry. Instead, I slowly stand up and walk out the door. But instead of walking to the nurse's office, I walk out of the school, across the yard, to the pine tree that just yesterday we sat next to.

* * *

How could it have been only yesterday that I saw him lying on the ground as the sky split open? As we sat side by side, his unrelenting faith flashing across his face.

The image of him wiping away his tears when I told him my mind was made up. That was how we ended things. *Those were my final words to him. He deserved so much more.*

I sit down and let all the tears out.

How? How could this happen to someone like him?

Life was so unnecessarily cruel!

I scream at the sky, "How dare you, God!"

The same sky that had opened and shown his glory.

I sit there next to the pine tree for a while and let myself cry, allowing myself to feel the pain and loneliness that has crept in now that my only friend is gone.

Out of the corner of my eye, I see a shadow move across the ground.

My skin goes cold. The hairs on the back of my neck rise.

I jump up, wiping my face with the sleeve of my sweatshirt, sure I've been found by a teacher. But when I spin around—

No one's there.

The wind rustles the pine needles and the birds start chirping.

I'm seeing things again.

First the creature in my room. Then on the bus. And now this.

Maybe the news about Joshua is messing with my head.

I'm not sure what that was. Maybe grief, maybe my imagination. It doesn't matter.

I shove the feeling down, burying it beneath everything else I don't want to deal with.

The pain. The fear. The confusion.

This ache will be over soon.

I tell myself that like a promise.

I'll be with Joshua again.

So why does it still hurt?

Maybe it's because I had started accepting the idea that maybe living isn't so bad if you have a friend like Joshua. There was a little part of me that knew if I had just seen Joshua one more time, I might have stayed.

I get up, wipe the grass off of me, and start walking back into the school.

My second class of the day is about to start.

I'm not sure why I even bother with school today. I could just leave. *No one would notice.*

However, I'm nervous to change anything up out of fear they will catch on to my plans and try to stop me.

I walk into the classroom and hear whispering, but this time it isn't about me.

One of the kids in my class found out what happened to Joshua through his mom who worked at the same place as Joshua's mom.

Stories spread quickly in small towns.

Jenny and Jessica are in this class with me, and when they look over, their faces are stricken with shock.

What happened to Joshua? I have to know.

I turn to the kid whispering with his friend next to me and ask him if he knows.

The kid's name is Tom, and he looks hesitant to share with me, but his friend nudges him, saying, "Go on, they were friends."

It's a rare moment when they put aside their dislike for me and treat me as a human.

Tom shifts awkwardly, but finally starts talking.

"Joshua's dad came home drunk last night," Tom says, barely above a whisper. "He, uh… he lost his job. He started yelling at Joshua's mom. Then he… he shoved her. Joshua tried to stop him."

He swallows hard. "His dad threw him down and started hitting him. Over and over."

Tom stares at his desk. "His mom called the cops, but… it was too late."

I feel sick to my stomach, my toast from breakfast threatening to come up.

How could his father kill him?

Joshua didn't deserve any of that.

Tears start streaming freely down my face again.

Tom tells me he's sorry, and so does his friend.

All the kids look at me, and for the first time, I feel seen by them. Their eyes filled with sadness.

I'm shocked to see Jenny stand up from her desk and walk over. She hesitates for a moment before wrapping her arms around me.

I numbly hug her back, too stunned to do anything else.

"I'm so sorry, Samantha," she whispers.

She pulls away awkwardly. Jessica looks like she wants to do the same but buries her head in her arms instead. I had hurt her the most when our friendship ended.

As Jenny walks back to her desk, a small warmth tries to push its way into my heart.

Death has a strange way of bringing people together, or pushing them apart.

I sit down and stare at the desk, my heart breaking in half when I notice something etched into the corner in jagged handwriting: Joshua 1:9.

Images of Joshua flood my mind. I don't even know what that verse says, but the second I see his name, I'm back walking toward the pine tree, watching him worship God.

His eye still swollen from the abuse, yet his face radiating peace.

I remember how his face lit up when he talked about God's faithfulness. He smirked, like he knew a secret the rest of us didn't.

He was brave.

He made me feel like I could be brave, too.

Feeling the stares of my classmates pressing in, I realize I can't do this. I can't sit here and pretend everything is fine.

I stand up and walk out of the classroom.

Out of the school.

And this time, I don't go to the pine tree.

I walk straight into the woods, tears streaming down my face as I ignore the memory forcing its way through: Joshua begging me to stay.

My plan just moved up.

The pain is too much, and I won't let it stay.

CHAPTER 19

"My sheep hear my voice, and I know them, and they
follow me. I give them eternal life, and they will
never perish, and no one will snatch them out of
my hand. My Father, who has given them to me, is
greater than all, and no one is able to snatch them
out of the Father's hand. I and the Father are one."

JOHN 10:27-30 ESV

As I stand here in the cold, dark woods, a stillness settles heavily over the trees.

The birds are no longer chirping.

I can hear my own heavy breathing. It's as if all of creation knows something is about to happen, and it's waiting. No one dares to move.

Reaching into my bag with shaky hands, I pull out a bottle of medication. Keeping it with me always felt safer than risking my mother finding it.

She had surgery last year and never used all of the pain medication. One day, she carelessly threw the bottle into the trash instead of flushing it down the toilet. Between that and the random pills I've found in our medicine cabinet, I hope it's enough of a potent mixture to put me out of my misery.

This has to work.

My hands won't stop shaking, no matter how much I try.

This is what I want. There's nothing to fear.

I eye the bottle and feel a coldness creep into my bones.

Yes, I'm in the middle of the woods on a cool spring day, but this is something different.

This feels like it's consuming me from the inside out.

My teeth begin to chatter, and I start to shake, my body in complete rebellion against my mind.

I hear a loud voice, booming in a demanding tone.

"DO IT NOW, SAMMY! TAKE THE PILLS AND END YOUR MISERY!"

It's coming from inside my head, but it isn't my voice.

I'm losing my mind, I tell myself.

I sit down on the cold ground, taking a moment before I use the pills. I pause, looking back on my life: my great childhood, my best friends Jenny and Jessica, then Stephen, and finally Joshua.

Just the thought of Joshua brings up fresh hurt and reminds me why I need to end things earlier than planned.

We were supposed to have one more day together.

The coldness returns. My arms begin to tingle and goosebumps rise on my skin. My stomach churns and the toast from breakfast once again threatens to rise. The shaking intensifies. My body convulses on the ground.

And again, the voice booms, resounding in my mind.

"DO IT NOW, SAMMY,"

it growls.

"YOU ARE MISERABLE AND ALONE. END YOUR LIFE. NOW!"

I stand up and grab my head in agony, the voice snarling on and on.

What's going on? Who is speaking to me? Isn't this my plan? To end my life and go to Heaven? Isn't this what I want? Then why does this voice make me second-guess everything? Who is so angry with me that they want me to die?

A single word floats into my mind: *thief.*

A scripture from long ago that I memorized in Sunday School comes back to me: *"The thief comes only to steal and kill and destroy. I came that they may have life and have it abundantly."*

I repeat it again, but this time out loud. It feels important—necessary to say. As the words leave my mouth, they resonate in my soul, like a light switch flips on.

"The thief comes only to steal and kill and destroy. I came that they may have life and have it abundantly."

Suddenly, I hear multiple voices in my head. It feels like a battle is raging for my soul.

The growling voices boom in unison:

"YOU ARE WORTHLESS, SAMMY! GIVE UP!"

But there's a new voice now. A quiet one I have to strain to hear. And when it speaks, warmth floods my bones:

"You are loved, Sammy."

Back and forth the voices go.

"YOU ARE NOTHING SAMMY! YOU NEED TO KILL YOURSELF TO ESCAPE THIS MISERY! THERE IS NO HOPE FOR YOU!"

"You are a child of God, Sammy, whom I love and died for. I have a plan for you. I am your hope and future."

I'm thrown to the ground, the agony of the voices ripping through my body.

Jesus, make it stop, I beg.

The growling voice starts to rise again—but something stirs inside me.

A strength that doesn't come from me.

My voice trembles, but with a courage I know can only come from one person, I cry out:

"STOP!"

My mind goes silent. The growling voice doesn't speak again, but neither does the quiet one.

I grab the pill bottle. My hands steady, I slowly open it, determined to end the voices once and for all. I pour them into my hand. A few fall to the ground, and I fumble around looking for them. I'll need every last bit to make sure this works.

As I search for the pills, something catches my eye half-buried in the dirt.

It's brown and blends in perfectly. I brush away more of the earth, and my eyes go wide when I see what it is. The rest of the pills drop from my hand.

It's the journal from my first trip to Heaven.

I pick it up and open to the first page. But instead of my handwriting, I'm met with someone else's.

Dear Sammy,

I found this in my room. I don't know how it ended up here. I probably shouldn't have opened it… sorry! But I felt like I needed to. I loved reading about your adventures in Heaven. I feel like God wants me to write you a note. I'm not sure why, since I'll see you at school tomorrow. But I can't shake the feeling. I've been thinking about what you said before I left today. I know deep down you don't really want to leave. I've been praying for you all day. I won't stop. I'm really thankful for our friendship. It's only been a couple of days, but God has already used it to show me a lot. You've reminded me why life is worth living: helping people, being a friend to someone who needs one. Also, the thing I really wanted to tell you is this: The enemy is always going to be the loudest. But when he's yelling, listen for the other voice. It'll be quiet, but it will tell the truth. And the truth will set you free.

Your forever friend,
Joshua

P.S. Here's my favorite verse and not just because it's my name.

"Have I not commanded you? Be strong and courageous. Do not be frightened, and do not be dismayed, for the Lord your God is with you wherever you go." Joshua 1:9

How can this be?
A letter from Joshua… in my journal that I left in Heaven? And it ended up in his room?

I frantically read it again, my eyes misting as I whisper Joshua 1:9 over and over.

Be strong and courageous… the Lord your God is with you.

This couldn't all be a coincidence.

For the first time, my thoughts become clear.

His words about the quiet voice ring in my heart.

I heard it just a moment ago, in the middle of all the yelling.

And I recognized it.

I met him in Heaven.

He held me in his arms as I cried.

He took on all my pain, every last bit.

He died so I could live.

The realization hits me like a punch in the gut.

He died so I could live.

For the first time, I kneel on the forest floor and listen to the voice of truth.

I surrender it all.

"Jesus," I whisper. "I don't even know where to go from here. But I do know this: this life isn't mine to take."

Tears stream down my face.

"I don't know if things will ever get better, or if I'll ever be okay. But I want to trust you. I'm done trying to do this on my own. Please forgive me. Please take away my pain. Please help me."

I clutch the journal to my chest.

"I know you died for me. I believe you love me. Really love me. I want to live, Jesus. I want to live!"

I whisper one more time, "I want to live…" and I feel the weight of the chains of darkness fall off of me.

I lay there, weightless on the ground. My body no longer shakes.

Warmth fills me. I look up and suddenly, the sky begins to swirl. The clouds split open, and before me are thousands upon thousands of people clapping, cheering, and praising God.

"Glory! Glory to God!"

"He has saved Sammy!"

"Run your race Sammy, run your race!"

My mouth is left wide open in amazement and wonder. Then, I see the most beautiful sight: Jesus, Joshua, and Stephen standing together, laughing with joy.

Jesus, my Savior, my best friend. Standing there in all his glory, eyes burning with love, his face shining like the sun. A smile stretches across his face, and I'm struck again by the love he has for me. My eyes fill with tears. I lift my arms and start praising him for saving my life.

Joshua smiles his eye-crinkling smile and it's even more beautiful in Heaven. I hear his voice though his mouth doesn't move, "You're going to be okay, Sammy. I'm glad you got my note." He winks in true Joshua fashion.

I'm not sure if he can hear me, but I respond anyway. "Thank you, Joshua. You changed my life." And with that, I receive an even bigger grin.

He is home. He finished his race. He didn't give up, and because of his determination despite all of the pain, I am sitting here alive. Gratitude fills me. "Your death won't be in vain, Joshua."

I see Stephen watching me. He smiles like a proud brother does when his little sister wins her first game. I know he's proud of me. I'll be reunited with him one day, but today isn't that day.

I can finally see clearly that I have a life worth living. And I know God will be leading me every step of the way, with all of Heaven and his people cheering me on.

I gaze up into the eyes of my Savior once more. He is the glory that waits for me. I thank God that I got to see a glimpse. He is my hope, and that hope will carry me forward. One day, I will walk with him again in eternity, living life as it was meant to be, working and playing with those we love, without any sin or pain.

Jesus smiles once more, and I hear the quiet voice in my mind:

"You are my beloved."

The clouds close up, and the sky returns to normal in a flash. I am left lying on the ground, feeling anything but normal.

My life was changed in that moment. The sadness lifted, and hope took its place.

When I walk out of the woods today, I don't know what will be waiting for me, but I'm not scared anymore.

I will pray for those who have hurt me.

I will forgive my family and friends.

And I will love as Jesus loved me when he died on the cross so I wouldn't have to.

And I will finally tell someone what's going on.

Jesus will give me the strength to do it, and I believe he will take care of me.

I get up and wipe the dirt from my pants.

I walk out of the woods with my head held high and a heart full of peace.

I'm walking out with a new heart and a glimpse of glory that will carry me all the way to eternity.

CHAPTER 20

*"Be kind to one another, tenderhearted, forgiving
one another, as God in Christ forgave you."*

Ephesians 4:32 esv

Standing on the outskirts of the woods, I see the pine tree that left my heart aching. It looks different now. It holds the secrets of two friends who stood on the edge of life and death. It stood witness to the glory of God.

How many kids will walk by this tree and never know the power that was once here?

I glance at the clock. Lunch is over, and my next class will be starting soon. There's no way I can go back to school after what happened. *I wonder if the teachers have noticed I'm gone. Did they call my mother?*

I need to go home. I'm a little anxious about what will be waiting for me there, but I will pray and trust that God is truly with me. Come Monday, I'll talk to the school counselors. It's time to tell someone the truth.

Exhaustion washes over me, the battle in the woods still heavy on my body, but there is a gentle strength holding me together. I know I need time to heal. Between my parents' divorce and Joshua's death, I need space to mourn.

It's a long walk home, but I need the time to mentally prepare and pray. My mother isn't working today, and when she sees me walk through the door earlier than I'm supposed to, it won't be pretty.

The unknown waits for me, but I walk with a sense of peace. Deep down, I know I'll be okay no matter what. Jesus has shown me that my life is held in the hands of God, and I trust he'll be with me through everything.

I'm still a little scared about facing life and its hardships, but I'm ready to fulfill my purpose.

Just like Joshua did.

Maybe things will turn around. I have hope.

I see my house in the distance, and my heart starts to pound. *Lord, be with me,* I whisper.

A bunny darts out from a bush and stops in front of me. It stares, tilting its head, before vanishing back into the greenery. It reminds me of the day Joshua and I sat by the pine tree—the bunny that surprised us then. He thought it was the coolest thing. This bunny feels like a sign. A small reassurance of what I need to do.

There is a host of angels and of people who love me, cheering me on. My heart aches thinking about Joshua. I will miss him. He faced more than I ever have, but he never gave up.

I will face my mother today, and I will do it with strength and courage.

I step onto our perfectly manicured lawn. The landscaper must have come today. Such an immaculate yard, yet it doesn't match the hearts inside the house.

I walk through the red door, heart hammering, palms sweating.

What I find on the other side is not what I am expecting.

I expect to see my mother on the couch, watching the daytime news with a glass of wine, in her bathrobe. She expects perfection from everyone else but hides away from her problems.

Instead, I find her with her head in a book, tears flowing from her eyes, and a look of horror on her face. She is so engrossed in the book, she doesn't even hear me come in.

I'm focused on her tears and face that I don't immediately notice that the book isn't just any book.

It looks like my journal.

The journal that holds all my secrets, including the one about killing myself.

Fear fills me and my body goes cold. I grab my backpack and rip it open, praying this is a mistake and that my journal is inside.

But it isn't.

I'd left it on my nightstand.

Open.

To the last entry.

The one I never meant for anyone to read.

I need to say something, and quickly.

"Mother."

She quickly lifts her head, and with a look of shock on her face, she doesn't move or speak. Time slows down, and we're frozen in place. A final battle about to begin.

She finally stands up, still completely silent. Her face is white, and it looks like she has seen a ghost. Tears mist her red, swollen eyes and she walks toward me.

I'm not sure what I'm expecting to happen next, but I brace myself for the worst. I close my eyes, waiting for a slap across the face. My body goes tense as she gets closer.

And then she hugs me.

She hugs me so tight that I can barely breathe, and she says over and over again, "I'm so sorry, Sam. I'm so sorry, my baby girl."

Bursting into tears, I hug her back. I'm not sure if it's because of my parents' divorce, Joshua dying, or the fact that my mother is hugging me for the first time in two years and calling me *baby girl*. But I weep, and she does too. We stay like that for a long time before I finally pull away. I start to explain myself, but she interrupts me.

"Let me speak first, Sam. I owe you an apology." She grabs my hand and leads me to the couch, patting the seat next to her.

"Two years ago, your brother died, and I felt like I did too." Her voice breaks, the pain still raw. She clears her throat and presses on.

"I've battled depression most of my life, but when he died… I snapped. Everything I'd bottled up. The years of not getting help. It all came crashing down. I lost my mind. I don't know how else to put it. I didn't know how to process what I was feeling, so it turned into rage. It was the only way I felt in control. The only way I knew how to protect myself… how to survive the pain."

She pauses, then continues, "Through that, I pushed your father out of my life. He was never perfect, but he tried to help me. He was dealing with demons of his own, and they caught up to him. We both should've gotten help, but instead, we controlled what we could and took all our anger out on you. Deep down, I knew it wasn't okay. I knew it was abuse. It wasn't fair to you, and it wasn't right. I couldn't stop it, though. It just kept getting worse and worse. The shame I felt going to bed each night, I suppressed it, like I've done my entire life."

Her face is filled with remorse. Tears pour from her eyes as she looks into mine, begging me to understand.

She sighs shakily before going on. "I was walking by your room this morning when I felt a pull to go inside. That's when I saw the journal on your nightstand. I couldn't stop myself from reading it.

I thought it would fuel my fire to keep treating you this way, but what I read…"

She stops then, as the tears choke her throat. She swallows them down and continues.

"When I read that you planned on committing suicide, it was like this veil was removed from my eyes. I read the journal from beginning to end, over and over, and I wept. I begged God for forgiveness. Starving you, berating you, the yelling, the slapping… I couldn't believe I could do something like that to my own child. But I did. And I will have to live with that for the rest of my life."

She hugs me again. And I have nothing to say. I'm stunned.

"Oh, Sam, if I lost you too, I don't know what I would do. Promise me you won't do it. Promise me you'll stay. I'm so, so sorry. I already called the doctors and a therapist. I'm going to get help. I'm going to be the mom you deserve and need. I'm so sorry, Sam. I don't deserve any forgiveness from you, but I hope one day you will forgive me, for your sake, not mine."

She reaches for my hands, her voice trembling. "What I've done… what your father's done… don't let that stop you from living your life. I'll talk to him. And if he won't get help, we'll set boundaries. Real ones. I'll call my sister too. I pushed her away because I didn't want her to see what was happening, but she's been calling. She's been asking about you. She cares. I think… I think you should stay with her for a while, until I can get better. I'm so sorry, Sam."

My brain is trying to absorb everything she's telling me. *Can I trust what she's saying after all that's happened?*

The tables have turned. I have the power now. The power to destroy her like she destroyed me. But although my heart is still broken from all these years, the Lord has already begun to do a work in it. My heart is changing. Even though it might take a long time and a lot of work to repair our relationship, in this moment, I feel only sadness for her.

She is the one tormented.

I have been set free.

So I say the words that I know will release her from the guilt.

"I love you, Mom. And I forgive you."

She bursts into tears, and I tell her everything. I tell her about Joshua, about how I almost ended everything today. I tell her about the battle for my soul. Then I share what I haven't even written in my journal: what I saw in Heaven. I tell her about Jesus, how he is real. How Heaven is real. And that Stephen is there, waiting for us.

It doesn't matter if she believes me or not. I feel compelled to share it all.

She soaks in every word I say, her eyes lighting up.

And then, right there on that old, green, faded rug that's seen so much life, she gives her life to Jesus.

I lead her in prayer. I'm not sure exactly what to say, but I know it doesn't need to be complicated. She repeats after me: "Lord, I know I've made mistakes and that I'm not perfect. I ask for forgiveness for my sins. I believe that Jesus died on the cross for me, and I ask that he would come into my heart and transform me every day. Thank you for life and restoration. In Jesus' name. Amen."

We sit together for a long time, holding each other. We let the past melt away and a new life begin.

. . . .

That night, lying in bed, my mind swirls with the events of the day. I can't believe it all happened in a single day. My parents announcing their divorce, Joshua dying, Jesus setting me free from the darkness, and my mother apologizing and giving her life to Jesus.

So many emotions. Fresh pain rips through my chest thinking about my friend. *I don't know when that one will ever get easier.*

I can't process everything right now, but there will be time. My mother has already set up an appointment for me with a therapist, and tomorrow I'll be moving in with my aunt a few hours away. I'll finish the school year as a homeschool student. I need time to heal away from here, and my mother will be going through her own healing journey. She'll have support from doctors, therapists, and hopefully now the church.

There's still a lot of pain. The abuse won't disappear overnight. But we're taking steps.

She plans to tell my father everything once I'm safe at my aunt's. We're not sure how he'll react, but for once, my mother is putting my well-being first.

Everything is changing.

I put on some worship music that Joshua told me about. I lie there, letting the lyrics wash over me: *"Amazing grace, how sweet the sound…"*

Tomorrow, when I wake up, there won't be a countdown. No more waiting for the end. I've been given a new beginning, and I can do anything with it.

Peace fills my heart as I drift off to sleep, grateful for the boy who refused to give up.

Goodnight, Joshua. I'll see you again.

EPILOGUE

"And this is the promise that he made to us—eternal life."

1 John 2:25 esv

The fluorescent lights hurt my eyes, and the sterile air makes my insides churn, yet I still feel a sense of peace in this room. I smile, knowing it's almost time for me to go home. After all these years… *it's time.*

"Grams!"

The familiar shout breaks through my thoughts, followed by the sound of small feet pounding against the linoleum. My mischievous great-grandchildren come bounding into the hospital room. Five of them under the age of ten, practically tripping over each other in their rush to reach me.

Just behind them are my two grandchildren, each with their beautiful wives, now scolding the kids to behave. I tear up, like I always do, when I think about how my sweet daughter, Della, named her twin boys after two of the most important men I've ever known: Joshua and Stephen.

Two men I haven't seen in a long, long time.

A sliver of excitement stirs in my chest. I'll be seeing them again soon, along with my mother, who passed from cancer a decade after we reconciled. I was honored to hold her hand in those final days, watching her eyes shine as she whispered that she could see Stephen, safe in the arms of Jesus.

I wish we'd had more years together, but I'm grateful for that final decade full of grace, full of love.

My father passed on too, many years later. It took us a long time to reconcile, as he had many demons to battle. When my mother called him all those years ago, when I was just a fifteen-year-old girl, he told her he wanted nothing to do with her or me. The pain I felt didn't stop me from praying for him.

It took many, many years, but one day, I received a call from him. His wife, the one he left my mother and me for, had divorced him. He'd been battling addiction and was calling from rehab. That was the beginning of his journey to find Jesus. It was long, and it took us years to be in a good place, but we made it eventually.

My life was filled with pain and hardship. Even after I came to know Jesus, that didn't all go away. But there was also so much life, and so much goodness.

I smile, thinking about the light that came into my life: *my husband, Silas.* He passed into glory two years ago, and I have been missing him fiercely.

It feels like just yesterday that I met him. It was the first day of college (I had gotten into university), and he was my school tour guide. It sounds so cliché, but we fell in love hard and fast. It was a whirlwind romance, and we were married two years later.

Little Della came right after college. It made being a journalist a little difficult, but we made it work. She was our only daughter, after many attempts to have another. Those days were dark and trying on our marriage. After three miscarriages, we stopped trying. Della was more than enough. She kept our lives full and filled with joy.

Those years with Silas and Della are my fondest memories. It wasn't an easy life, and we experienced our fair share of loss and hardship. Our marriage barely survived in the early days, but we always pushed through, relying on God's strength.

As Della got older, I was able to travel more for work. Silas and Della joined me for many of those adventures. The places I've been. The people I've met. The stories I've gotten to tell. I choke up when I think back on my life, and how it was almost never possible because of a lie the conspirator told me when I was fifteen years old.

I shake my head and look around the room. *Life, indeed, was worth living.*

Della, my beautiful daughter, walks in last. She is graceful, aging so beautifully. She fills the room with brightness, her name always fitting her perfectly. *Noble.*

Her worried green eyes search my face as soon as she sees me. I send her a reassuring smile, but I know deep down this will be the final day I see my precious family… a family I almost never had.

They all surround my bed, but they make room for Della to sit in the chair beside me. She reaches out and takes my once-strong hand, now little more than bones.

"Hi, Mom. How are you feeling? You look great!"

I chuckle.

"Oh, Della. You know you're not supposed to lie to your mother."

I know I look far from great. I'm ninety-two years old, and every part of my body is either sagging or stretched thin over fragile bones. But I feel more alive now than I ever have. My soul is calling to the one who rescued it all those decades ago.

I take my time looking at each of these unique souls standing around my bed, memorizing their sweet faces one by one, before stopping to look my daughter in the eyes. A look of knowing shifts across her face. But before she can say anything, I take out a worn brown journal that was gifted to me a long, long time ago in a far-away place and turn to the first page.

The letter from Joshua is still there, stained with dirt and tears from that life-changing day in the forest.

"Have I ever told you the story of when I went to Heaven?"

ACKNOWLEDGMENTS

This book would not exist without my Savior and friend, Jesus. There were dark seasons in my life when I almost didn't listen to the voice of truth, but He never gave up on me. I am beyond grateful for the life-changing power of the cross.

My husband, Shane, believed in me from the very beginning and cheered me on every step of the way. Your encouragement gave me the push I needed every time I doubted myself.

My daughter, Birdi, you are one of the biggest reasons I kept going. Every time I wanted to give up, I thought of you. I wanted to show you that you can do hard things and that pursuing your dreams, even when it is scary, is always worth it.

I owe special thanks to Hannah Anders. Your thoughtful editing and insight challenged and sharpened me as a writer. This book would not be what it is without your talent and heart.

Thank you to Steve Kuhn for your excellence in formatting and for helping bring the cover to life.

To all the beta readers, family, and friends who read early drafts, asked about my progress, offered encouragement, and believed in me, I am deeply thankful. Your support meant more than you know.

And finally, to you, the reader. Thank you for holding this book in your hands. I pray this story brings you hope and shines a light in your life. May everything we do be done for the glory of the Lord. My deepest prayer is that this book leads hearts to the gospel and to the unshakable hope found in Jesus Christ.

DISCUSSION GUIDE

*These questions are designed to help you reflect more deeply
on Sammy's journey and on your own. They can be used
for personal reflection, journaling, or group discussion.*

1. Sammy begins her journey feeling hopeless and convinced that
   life isn't worth living. What emotions or experiences from your
   own life did this stir in you?

   Going Deeper: *Read Psalm 34:18. How does this verse remind
   you of God's closeness in times of pain? Write down one way you've
   seen Him meet you in a hard place.*

2. Joshua becomes an unexpected friend who listens and cares. How
   has friendship made a difference in your life? How might God
   be calling you to be a "Joshua" for someone else?

   Going Deeper: *Read Ecclesiastes 4:9–10. Who has God placed
   in your life to encourage you? And who might He be asking you to
   encourage this week? Reach out to one person.*

3. Sammy receives an invitation to Heaven and encounters Jesus
   in powerful ways. What stood out to you most in these scenes?
   How does the presence of Jesus bring healing and hope?

Going Deeper: *Read Matthew 11:28–30. In prayer, give one of your burdens to Jesus. Journal how it feels to entrust that weight to Him.*

4. Lies about worth, guilt, and shame often whisper louder than truth. Which lies does Sammy wrestle with that felt familiar to you? What truths from Scripture can replace them?

   Going Deeper: *Read Romans 8:38–39. Write out one lie you've believed and then write a truth from God's Word that speaks against it. Post the truth somewhere you'll see it often.*

5. Sammy's family is broken and complicated, yet moments of forgiveness and healing emerge. Why do you think forgiveness is so hard? How has God helped you forgive—or how is He still working on your heart?

   Going Deeper: *Read Ephesians 4:31–32. Think of one relationship where you need to extend grace. Pray for that person by name this week.*

6. Sammy learns that even in her lowest moments, God's light is still breaking through. Where have you seen light in your own seasons of darkness?

   Going Deeper: *Read John 1:5. Take a walk outside and reflect on how light always pierces through darkness. Thank God for the ways His light has shone in your life.*

7. By the end of the book, Sammy is faced with a choice: to give in to despair or to embrace hope. What does "a glimpse of glory" mean to you personally? How can you hold on to that hope in your own journey?

Going Deeper: *Read Jeremiah 29:11. Write down one area of your life where you need to hold on to hope. Pray over it and ask God to show you His purpose in that place.*

ABOUT THE AUTHOR

Shandi Carrier is a Jesus-loving writer passionate about telling stories that point to Christ and reveal the power of light overcoming darkness. A stay-at-home mom in New England, she finds inspiration in deep conversations, unexpected adventures, and the beauty of God's creation.

A Glimpse of Glory is her debut novel—born out of her own journey through pain, healing, and discovering God's unwavering love.

When she's not writing, Shandi can be found reading late into the night, watching the Red Sox with her husband, or adding new book ideas to the Notes app she swears she'll organize someday.

www.ingramcontent.com/pod-product-compliance
Lightning Source LLC
Chambersburg PA
CBHW050333110726
47899CB00007B/2479